MW01488032

NO
ONE
CALLS
ME
ROSIE

NO
ONE
CALLS
ME
ROSIE

JERROD R. DANIELS

www.ivyhousebooks.com

This is a work of fiction. The names, characters and places are a product of the author's imagination and any resemblance to actual events or persons, living or dead, is entirely coincidental.

PUBLISHED BY IVY HOUSE PUBLISHING GROUP
5122 Bur Oak Circle, Raleigh, NC 27612
United States of America
919-782-0281
www.ivyhousebooks.com

ISBN13: 978-1-57197-492-1
Library of Congress Control Number: 2008925573

Printed in the United States of America

To those who rescue

The question isn't who is going to let me;
it's who is going to stop me.

—AYN RAND
The Fountainhead

CHAPTER 1

Opening one eye, then the other, Rhonda Haynes checked the time. When the morning's first light had eased into the bedroom, her first impulse had been to jump up, but a gnawing dread kept her where she was. Finally, when the numerals on the digital clock showed seven o'clock, she knew she could stay there no longer.

Giving her sleeping husband a gentle pat on his bare buttocks, she pulled the sheet back over him and slipped out of the large bed. She quickly tied her hair back with a clip, grabbed her silk robe off the chest at the foot of the bed, and headed downstairs.

Tying the robe's sash tighter as she entered the kitchen, she walked straight to the radio on the black marble countertop. She wanted to hear the latest commentary on the evening's upcoming events and didn't have to wait long. Reaching for a coffee cup, she listened as the familiar voice of the announcer enthusiastically reminded his audience about the awards show. She adjusted her hair clip even tighter and leaned against the countertop, while her announcer buddy explained the importance of the day to anyone tuned to Country FM 108.

"Good morning, everyone. And if you're having a really great day, it's because you must be in or darn near Nashville, capital of the great state of Tennessee and the capital of country music. This is Sonny Boyd Everett on Country FM one-o-eight welcoming you to the greatest sounds around and to what's without a doubt shaping up to be one of the biggest days in the whole history of country music.

"I don't have to remind you that the Best in Country Music Awards are being handed out tonight out at the Opry House. This is always a big night in the music world for millions of fans. But tonight's awards have taken on a real special twist this year with three of the top gals in the business nailing down all three slots for Entertainer of the Year.

"Tonight, for the first time *ever*, my friends, it's ladies only. The legendary Rhonda Haynes, last year's winner Okalene Harris, and this year's surprise megastar, India Robbins. All battling it out for the top prize. All week long you've seen the nominees interviewed on television and heard them on radio talk shows. But this morning we're going to let you in on the real reason they've been nominated for Entertainer of the Year. And it's no great secret. All I have to do is play the fabulous songs that have gotten these gifted performers to the very top of their business. Then you can decide for yourself who's going to walk away with the big one, if you haven't already.

"And how about we start this morning's show with one of the greatest hits Rhonda Haynes ever had. Let's listen to 'He's You All Over Again.'"

Beyond Music City, once long ago heralded as the Athens of the South, past limestone bluffs and rolling fields dotted with cedar trees and gray wooden barns leaning slightly to one side, twenty-five miles east of Nashville, off an interstate exit marked "Hooten Hollow," was the home of Rhonda Haynes, for years known as the undisputed Queen of Country Music.

Her farm, Honeysuckle Haven, was located three miles north of Hooten Hollow, a town named for Confederate General John Fransworth Hooten, who died in his sleep at the Battle of Stones River two hours before the battle actually began, a fact usually forgotten in local tales of the great struggle. Getting to Honeysuckle Haven required going through Hooten Hollow, population 4,857. Crossing the abandoned railroad tracks on the outskirts of town and then passing the old depot, long ago converted to a storehouse for the Street Department, the town's main road, two-lane Highway 51, was fronted by five used car lots, the Piggly Wiggly supermarket, a Dairy Queen, Wig City—featuring the popular Rhonda Haynes model in her signature shade of red—and Toot 'n Tell 'Em, a drive-in still featuring car hops.

The only point of interest daring to refer to any other star was Miss Dimple's School of Charm and Baton. Outside the front door of Miss Dimple's studio was a large digital clock permanently stopped and showing 3:30 A.M., August 16, 1977, the official time and date of Elvis Presley's death. Miss Dimple, whose real name was Katie Darnell, was a Mississippi girl who had moved to Hooten Hollow several years earlier with an undisclosed motivation and who had been to Las Vegas three times to see The King. She'd managed to snare two of the white scarves the sweating entertainer frequently tossed to his frantic audience. Both of those scarves were kept in a large plastic bag in her safe deposit box at the First National Bank. When asked by visitors about the curious time on the clock, Miss Dimple explained and was always quick to tell them she was also a "long-time personal friend of Rhonda Haynes."

North of town the pavement widened to three lanes as Highway 51 approached Honeysuckle Haven. That improvement had been made a few years earlier to accommodate heavy traffic, particularly frequent tour buses in the late spring and summer months, when Rhonda Haynes' home was a "must-see" for the thousands of often reverent, always colorful fans who made the pilgrimage to Music City from all over the world.

Honeysuckle Haven fronted the highway for almost a mile, and every foot was enclosed by a moss-covered stacked stone fence characteristic of the region. Despite the farm's name, the only honeysuckle in sight was the red variety growing over the stone fence and practically enveloping the large mailbox at the entrance to the farm. Rhonda told any guests who might ask that most of the honeysuckle was down along the winding, spring-fed creek that ambled across the rear of the farm. On both sides of the driveway, lined with towering cedar trees, were pastures where her prized Tennessee walking horses and Kentucky thoroughbreds stood and frequently gazed back at the tour buses lined up along the highway.

"Oh, look, Horace. That black horse over there, the one on the far right, has a stick or something on his stomach. I'm going to get a picture. Hon, move over a little bit."

"For God's sake, Lazetta. That's his wienie. Take a picture of something else. You'd think you'd never been on a farm or even been out of Valdosta before in your life."

At the far end of the driveway, fully visible from the highway, was a two-story antebellum mansion with a bright-red tin roof and six towering white columns—home to Rhonda Haynes for almost fifteen years. The main part of the house was built in 1857 by one of Andrew Jackson's relatives, whose slaves built the stone fences. The singing star had added numerous barns and horse stables over the years.

These structures stood away from the house behind a small rise and were not visible from the highway. But they were described in great detail over the tour bus microphones to the fans who absorbed every word.

"Estelle's cousin said she'd heard you could honestly eat off the stable floors, they're so clean. And each horse has its own shower. She swears."

Each year during Country Music Fans Week festivities, Rhonda Haynes opened Honeysuckle Haven to the devout public for one spectacular day and greeted each awestruck visitor at the door herself.

"Welcome to my world," she graciously told the fans who entered her home on that always very special day.

CHAPTER 2

It was still early morning on the day of the Best in Country Music Awards. The mistress of Honeysuckle Haven let her husband, Roger, sleep a little longer while she prepared their usual breakfast. She made what she always referred to as "Mama's scrambled eggs" and at the last minute threw in the necessary diced onions and green peppers along with some grated cheese, something she had watched her mother do many times years before. Quickly, she glanced through the entertainment section of the morning newspaper to see if anything new had been written about the evening's awards.

Satisfied nothing more had been said by any savvy music industry insider than what had been prophesized in the days before, she called through the intercom from the kitchen to announce breakfast was ready. Wearing only a terry-cloth robe and his favorite fleece-lined moccasins, Rhonda's husband eventually joined her at the round, glass-top breakfast table in the small room just off the kitchen.

"I'm meeting Avery and Dusty and a few of the musicians at the studio right after we're finished here," she said as soon as her husband was seated. Avery Springer was her manager, and Dusty Harmon was a songwriter who just happened to be her former husband. "Dusty's got a couple of songs to pitch, and this is as good a time as any. If I sit around here, I'll start stripping wallpaper with my teeth or worse. I'm as edgy as a barn cat stalking a big rat."

As he slowly poured cream into his second cup of coffee, he was confident she had probably put off telling him about her plans as long as she could. Anything concerning Dusty Harmon always made him leery, especially if Rhonda was involved. "You know damn well this thing with Dusty will probably be just another waste of your time," he responded. Dusty had been Rhonda Haynes' second husband for exactly twenty-seven months back in the late seventies, not counting the three months it took to get the divorce. In keeping with Tennessee law, Rhonda had merely cited "irreconcilable differences," also referred to as "no questions asked" or "none of your damn business," as she preferred to think of it, as the grounds for the divorce. Within two months of the final decree she released *Irreconcilable Differences* on Athena Records. Like the marriage, the record didn't fare too well, though it didn't take quite as long to reach its demise.

Without responding to her husband's warning, Rhonda picked up a crust of toast and pushed it through the bars of the large birdcage, hoping to silence the two cockatiels that were screeching for attention.

"Why you let that mangy twerp keep calling and hanging around anytime he wants to, I'll never understand," Roger said as he finished the last of the eggs. Chasing the eggs with a large sip of coffee, he continued and tried to stay calm. "Trouble's all that ever comes of it. You above all people should know that."

She appreciated his effort to sound sensible, even objective, about someone who had long been a source of controversy in her life. Now age thirty-eight, Dusty Harmon was ten years younger than Rhonda, and she occasionally liked to playfully tease her husband about her ex-husband's "youth and vitality." In her private world she had been Mrs. Roger Keithe for more than six years, having waited five years before remarrying after her divorce from Dusty. Anytime Roger brought up the age difference between Rhonda and her second husband, she just smiled and winked at him, as if fondly remembering "that boy," as Roger called him.

Finally, Rhonda offered a reply from across the table. "I told you he only wants me to listen to a couple of songs he's written and that's all. His songs are all it ever is where I'm concerned. Besides, after last night what makes you think I could even want to see a man for any other reason any time soon?" She laughed, reached across the table and stroked his hand. She was referring to the marathon lovemaking session that had begun in their new hot tub and ended in the middle of their custom-built waterbed.

"When Dusty's got his head on straight, he can put together some really great lyrics. That's a proven fact, more than once, and you have to admit it," she said. "'Backing Out of Love' didn't do too badly for me a few years ago. In case you've forgotten, sweet cakes, that song sold over two million copies and had a lot to do with getting me the CMA award that year." Two years after their divorce, on her birthday, Dusty sent her a dozen pale pink rosebuds—her favorite—along with a tape he had made of himself singing "Backing Out of Love." She loved the roses and the country music world loved the song, enough to vote her "Best Female Vocalist" in 1981. That song and the award came at a time when many people in the music business thought Rhonda might be on her way to becoming a much respected memory, no longer worthy of the prestige and accolades she had long commanded as the Queen of Country Music in the sixties and seventies. But that was in 1981, and once again Rhonda felt she was in need of a hit, something big to show the close-knit powers-that-be in Nashville that she was still the Queen.

Her latest album, *Definitely Rhonda*, and its top selling single "Yesterdays Are Best Left That Way" resulted in her nomination for Entertainer of the Year, but she knew she had to follow up quickly with another impressive hit. In her mind she was convinced it would take two back-to-back successes to maintain her status.

"And it says right here," she said, referring to her horoscope in the newspaper, "that 'someone from the past will bring you a message.' And it says my moon is entering a phase with Jupiter, whatever the hell that means." She folded the paper with an I-guess-that-shows-you gesture. "What more assurance should you need?" she joked.

While her husband reached once more for the coffee urn on the far side of the table, Rhonda made a suggestion. "Why don't you go with me? We're meeting at Athena a little before noon, but won't be there too long. I also need to stop by Rivergate Mall for some make-up afterwards, but I'll just run in and run right out." In many ways unaffected by her fame, Rhonda always insisted on shopping for herself at the large mall north of Nashville. Delighted fans couldn't resist asking for her autograph and bought anything she touched but left behind. "We'll be back by four o'clock at the latest. I'll need plenty of time to get ready for the show this evening. We've got to go by Avery's house for a party beforehand, but I want to be at the Opry House no later than seven."

Whether it was the thought of the mall and the "run right in and run right out" promise he knew she couldn't keep, or the prospect of seeing Dusty Harmon, for whatever reason, Roger declined her offer. "No, you go ahead. Since it's raining, have Carl drive you in a little earlier. Traffic will be a mess," he advised. "I've got a new veterinarian coming to look at that bull. I want a second opinion on him. Operating on any bull is always risky." Carl Sutton was the resident jack-of-all trades and a trusted friend who helped around Honeysuckle Haven and drove the tour bus when Rhonda was on the road.

"Suit yourself," she replied. "Now get on out of here so I can haul these dishes to the kitchen and get going," she said and poked one last piece of toast into the birdcage. When she first came to Nashville, she had worked as a waitress and still insisted on doing certain things around the house for herself.

Bending over to give her husband a quick kiss on his head, she continued to needle him. "You fairly staggered when you got up to go to the bathroom during the night. You looked just like Amos McCoy in a hurry to help Little Luke put out a fire. Better go on up and take a long hot soak."

"It sure as hell wasn't Little Luke's fire I was putting out last night," he said and gave her a swat on her behind as he left the room. "Think I just might relax a little longer. Reading the newspaper should do the trick." He took the paper off the table and placed it under his arm. "Give Avery my best and tell him to have the bourbon in ready supply tonight."

Returning upstairs, she used both hands to adjust the clip in her hair. "Wonder if I ought to get it cut this afternoon after all," she mumbled to herself. The week before, she and Ruth Staggs, a friend who helped her with her wardrobe and hair, decided Rhonda needed to come on stage at the award show and make a bold statement. "With your red hair in full blaze," Ruth had said, "making a perfect frame around the most perfect skin in the business and green eyes God had meant for a cat." *Anyway,* Rhonda thought as she entered the bedroom, *Ruth will be here when I get back, and my hair will be her problem then.*

The plan was for her friend and personal assistant to bring three outfits for Rhonda to choose from. Each creation had been designed to remind everyone in the industry and the millions in the huge television audience that Rhonda Haynes was still a force to be reckoned with. The lady still had it all. The looks. The voice. And, most of all, she had that rare, almost regal quality called presence.

When she reached the pink bedroom with its soft, floral wallpaper, the deep carpet she loved to dig her toes into, and her large canopy bed, she was pleased to see the maid had already straightened the bed and the room. Ruth Staggs was the only person Rhonda ever wanted around when she was in the process of dressing for a concert, or any other occasion for that matter. Rhonda felt particularly so on that day. It was one of the few times when she didn't like being stared at by anyone, even her husband.

Off the bedroom was another room containing four racks, two on each side wall, one over the other, on which Rhonda's wardrobe of the moment was hung. On the racks hung her neatly arranged dresses, slacks, blouses, shirts, skirts, and light jackets. Her formal clothes were kept in a separate part of the suite altogether. Passing through the room, she entered another smaller room with an entire wall of built-in drawers for lingerie and sweaters. On the other wall were waist-high racks for dozens of pairs of shoes and boots. One interviewer touring the home had referred to Rhonda as "country music's Imelda Marcos" after seeing the star's dressing area. Above the shoes were several shelves for hats, although she rarely wore one, not wanting to "hide" her hair.

Only when she rode one of her horses would she tie back her hair with a scarf or bandanna. At the end of the clothes racks was a large dressing table and oversized bathroom, also in pink. Across the hall from their bedroom, Roger had the same arrangement in hunter green, though not as elaborate.

After sitting down before the large mirror over the dressing table, she picked up the pink telephone and called down to the stable, hoping to find Carl Sutton. "Carl, there you are. I'll be dressed and at the front door in about thirty minutes. Getting prepared to see an ex-husband doesn't require anything too special. Tonight's a whole other story. Will that work for you? Roger insists we leave early because of the rain and traffic. Good. See you in thirty minutes."

Following another quick trip back through the two rooms of clothes and elaborate accessories, she quickly dressed. When she finally turned to leave the bedroom, she stopped before the almost wall-sized, gilt-edged mirror to admire her body. Though she was gently pushing fifty, she felt she had never looked better. She quickly decided on a billowing white crepe blouse, one of her favorites. She knew the skin-tight silk faded blue jeans showed every curve in her perfect butt, tight thighs, and long legs. Turning before the mirror one more time, she put both hands on her hips, her long nails nearly meeting over her flat stomach.

"Eat your heart out, Okie Harris," she said and added, "bitch." With that she walked out of the pink cocoon, down the stairs, and out the front door, where Carl and the car were waiting. The rain had slackened off considerably, so she made the dash from between the white columns to the car without waiting for Carl to bring an umbrella.

"Sit still, Carl," she said as she slid into the backseat. "I won't melt. Though it won't do these silk pants much good," she added, checking her hair in the mirror to see if the run to the car had shaken anything loose. "Everything's fine," she announced to herself and settled back into the burgundy leather upholstery of the new charcoal-gray Cadillac, which at her insistence did not have tinted windows. "My fans want to see me in this thing, and I want to be seen," she had explained to the car dealer.

When they were purchasing the car, she and Roger had a brief difference of opinion at the Cadillac dealership in Brentwood, a wealthy Nashville bedroom community. Rhonda had insisted on a pink Cadillac with white leather interior. However, Roger gently persuaded her to change her mind. "Rhonda, if you drive around in a pink Cadillac, people will think you're selling Mary Kay cosmetics."

She immediately thought better of the idea and gave in. When the order was finally placed, the colors were charcoal-gray with a deep burgundy leather interior and a list of extra equipment Rhonda observed "must rival the spec sheet for that space shuttle."

"Carl, first we're going to the studio. Dusty's meeting all of us there. Then I need to make a quick run to Rivergate," she said. "But, for God's sake, make sure my carcass is back at home by four o'clock and no later. I promised Roger, and he's always right about those things."

"You got it, Rhonda," Carl replied and eased the royal carriage down the long driveway. He then nodded as she repeated what she had earlier promised her husband.

"We shouldn't be at the studio too long. And I'll just take a minute or two at Rivergate, I swear. But I'll need you to go with me at the mall, just so I won't get waylaid by anyone. You know I can't say no to anyone. You'll just have to do that for me. We'll do our good-gal-bad-guy thing." Once Carl had to drag her out of a flea market, as she described it, when everyone within a hundred yards of Rhonda demanded a pair of sunglasses just like the ones she had selected.

She was also determined the stay at Athena Studios would be short, especially if Dusty was in one of his "moods with horns," as she referred to his darker side. The meeting had to be short and strictly business, of that she was certain. There had been only a few truly significant men in Rhonda Haynes' life, husbands included. For years she refused to even discuss her first husband, only to say he had drowned, and wasted little time recalling her marriage to Dusty Harmon.

With Dusty the sex had been great. He had a smile that had always given her a twitch in her crotch. But the combination of his cocaine habit, often combined with his fondness for expensive brandy, was something else. Something that eventually destroyed her feelings for him. Bad habits may have overtaken Dusty, but no one and nothing but her desire to be someone controlled Rhonda. When it came to looking out for herself, Rhonda needed no one to tell her who was in charge. That's the way it had always been for her for as long as she could remember. Always.

Sitting back in the soft leather and heading for Nashville, she thought about her husband. Roger Keithe was different. He gave her the stability she had never known could exist. For the first time in her life she was confident a man loved her as much as she loved him, needed her as much as she needed him. As she said in one of her favorite songs—one she often dedicated to her husband—"It don't get much better than that."

Sitting there and just watching the rain increase as it struck the windows of the car, she switched on the radio to FM 108.

The last few bars of Okalene Harris' "Too Soon" were ending. Rhonda took pleasure in once again hearing the reassuring voice of Sonny Boyd Everett. In the past she knew she could count on the well-respected disc jockey whenever she needed a favorable play for a song others might have initially considered as just perhaps not up to her standards. Turning up the volume slightly, she took comfort in her longtime friend's mellow drawl.

"As promised, that was another hit by Okie Harris," the announcer said, "another number one song, mind you—and just one more reason why she's a nominee tonight for Entertainer of the Year. If you're fortunate enough to have been with us today, at least since I came on at the crack of dawn, you've heard many great recordings, and each one is a most definite reason why Okalene Harris, India Robbins, and, yes, the legend herself, Rhonda Haynes, are the nominees tonight for what the Best in Country Music Awards without hesitation calls "the very top." The pinnacle. Numero uno. The best. These ladies simply are the best and nothing else needs to be said. Each one of these gals stands for the great talent and hard work in their industry. And we're all so very proud of each one of them. It's going to be quite a choice to make, but tonight hundreds in the Opry House and millions around the world will see the results of the voting by you, the fans. Well, enough from me for right now. Right after this commercial break, you'll hear from the relative newcomer to stardom, India Robbins, and her block-buster hit on both the country and pop charts, 'The Best You've Ever Had.'"

Not wanting to hear a commercial, much less her competition, Rhonda reached over and snapped off the radio. She had heard enough to get a feel of what was being said about the night's awards. Her thoughts drifted back to her own music and then to Dusty. *The same Dusty who gave sex a bad name, and it's got to be bad to be good,* she mused. The Dusty who would spend his last dime—or hers when he had the chance—on cocaine and fancy alcohol. The same Dusty who could stare the pants off an old maid schoolteacher, as Rhonda once remarked to a girlfriend.

But above all the Dusty who could write lyrics that "reached down to the bottom of your heart and French kissed your soul," as she had described it to him during their happier times. They were all Dusty and each one was trouble, guaranteed.

CHAPTER 3

The rain was much heavier than when Rhonda and Carl Sutton left Honeysuckle Haven. So when they arrived at Athena Studio, she waited for him to come around the car with the umbrella. Together they walked slowly across the parking lot trying to avoid puddles. Another car was in the place always reserved for her. From the dented fender and smashed bumper, her instincts told her it probably belonged to Dusty.

They entered the two-story building by the rear entrance marked "Private."

The studio was quiet. Rhonda dramatically threw open the door to Avery Springer's office and announced, "All right, you worthless jackasses, let's see a little respect!" Someone responded immediately with a high-pitched rendition of Aretha Franklin's "R-e-s-p-e-c-t." Athena Records' top star had entered the room.

As president of the record company for over twenty years and throughout Rhonda Haynes' association with the label, Avery Springer insisted on being present when his number one talent was in the building for any reason. The small group in his office that day included Bill Pete Tucker, Athena's publicity chief; Scott Satterfield, Rhonda's longtime personal advisor; and Dusty Harmon. There were no women present, just the way the studio boss knew his star preferred, except during a recording session when back-up singers were essential.

Walking directly to the studio head, she draped both arms around Avery's neck, gave him a quick kiss on his grinning mouth, and without pausing walked over to Dusty, who was slouched in an overstuffed chair and taking in his ex-wife's entrance. Not expecting him to rise from the chair, she bent over, gave him a kiss on one cheek and said, "Dusty, you know I loved those roses." She was referring to the most recent dozen pink rosebuds he had sent her along with the message about wanting to have the meeting. What she didn't tell him was that she had tossed the roses and the note before Roger could see either of them. Just to keep the peace, she admitted to herself at the time.

With her gracious gesture toward Dusty, everyone else in the room relaxed. There had been too many Rhonda-Dusty blow-ups in the past, and everyone knew there was always the potential for another one when the two of them were around each other for any length of time.

Tall, skinny Bill Pete Tucker jumped up from the worn leather sofa and wrapped his long arms around the lady of the hour. "Congrats, babe," he said and gave her shoulders a soft squeeze.

"Now just hold on, Bill Pete," she stated dramatically. "It's not over yet by any means, and you damn know it. Anybody with both sides of his brain working knows Okie Harris is probably still out humping for votes, and the fact all the votes are already counted doesn't mean crap to that one. She makes the rest of us look like Campfire Girls." Addressing the others in the room, she asked, "Did any of you see her on television the other day with that grinning con artist who calls himself an evangelist? Now that takes nerve for both of them to pull that off." She paused while they laughed. "Now I wouldn't entirely write off little India by any means, but the one and only Okalene Harris is the only real competition this evening if my instincts and my horoscope this morning are worth a tinker's damn."

Everyone laughed. Avery Springer reminded the group about the main competition. "Don't forget the time Okie Harris, mind you, first runner up in the Miss Oklahoma contest several years ago, showed up on that early morning country music television show in town wearing a blouse cut so low the station's cameras only showed her from the neck up." Again, laughter, even from the usually laid-back Dusty. "I have it on good report that the station manager later admitted it didn't look just right to follow the national anthem and a brief 'Word with our Lord' with those famous knockers singing 'Strictly Personal.' That's when the station manager issued a dress code for the early morning show and made sure Okalene Harris received two copies."

A deadpan Bill Pete remarked, "Early morning Nashville just wasn't ready for that act."

"Hell, Bill Pete, early morning Tijuana wouldn't be ready for that," Rhonda replied. "That woman must be the fast food of sex." Enjoying the jokes at her rival's expense, she continued. "That girl's done everything but put up arches and install a drive through. Hell, and I'm not lying, Buddy Arnold swears that during a performance in Vegas, old Okie actually stuck her butt behind the curtain and never missed a note, while her boyfriend jump started her battery right there in full view of everybody backstage."

Before the laughter ended, Rhonda broke in, "I don't have a whole lot of time, so let's get this thing cranked up. Dusty, let me give you a quick gut reaction to what you've brought today and get back to you, if there's any one of them that's got some possibilities. Fair enough?"

For the first time Dusty, who had been carefully taking in the entire scene, finally spoke. He slowly extracted himself from the huge chair and replied, "Rhonda, that's not a problem. All I thought was that you might be interested and then you might not. It could be good for both of us, and it only works if that's the way it is."

For the first time since entering the room Rhonda focused solely on her ex-husband. He looked great, torn jeans and all. He sounded straight, which was a relief. She couldn't avoid noting his shaggy brown hair and deep brown eyes looked just as seductive as ever.

"Let's do it," Avery said, emerging from behind his desk. "I've already got Dusty's tape cued up in Studio B, so let's go in there and listen to what he's got to say."

Taking the cue from their boss, everyone moved toward the door Bill Pete held open for Rhonda. She then led the procession two doors down the familiar hallway, its walls covered with framed gold records, many of them hers.

Before Avery could give the studio sound engineer a sign to start the tape, Dusty had a few words of introduction. "Rhonda, I know I probably told you I was just bringing two songs, but at the last minute I hitched a third one on the tape. Just to let you know I'm not trying to take advantage or anything, today of all days. I realize what it means to you. It means a lot to all of us."

"I appreciate the warning, Dusty," she said, knowing he would never really stop trying to take advantage of anyone.

With everyone seated Avery pointed to the engineer sitting behind the large plate-glass window, and the tape began immediately. With Dusty singing and accompanying himself on a guitar, just as he had on many nights when they were married and at home between concert tour engagements, the first song played to a small audience, in all actuality an audience of one. It was an upbeat number entitled "Two Steps Back from the Edge." It went well, but the general reaction, as revealed on the faces of those listening, was ho-hum.

Knowing him as she did, Rhonda realized Dusty had anticipated that reaction and had purposely put that song on the tape first. She supposed he intended it to contrast with the second song, which he quietly said was his personal favorite. It was entitled "Loving in Your Lying Arms."

> *All this time*
> *You've been deceiving me,*
> *Leaving me to think you were mine.*
> *I saw nothing but loving*
> *In your smile,*
> *The passion in your eyes,*
> *Longing warmth in your sighs.*
> *Now I've found out*
> *Where the truth really is.*
> *I've been loving*
> *In your lying arms.*

"Now that kind of grabs me where it counts," Rhonda broke in as the song ended. "Avery, ask him to start the tape again back at the beginning of this last one."

They all listened again. Rhonda saw that Dusty's lyrics had everyone under his spell, but she chose not to show her own reaction.

Scott Satterfield, always the perfectionist, freely offered his impression when the second playing was finished. "I like it. Like it a lot. You might want to shorten the title. Maybe just 'Your Lying Arms,' but it probably will work either way. Just a thought."

"I don't know," Rhonda commented. "I sort of like the twist. In fact, I think it might be a line from an old song. You know something about lying and loving arms, but this is kind of unique. Dusty, why don't you and Scott get some musicians to work up the whole thing, and let's listen to it after that." Then her tone changed, became much more serious. "And, for God's sake, don't take a month to do it. Get moving on it as soon as you can." Her need for the big follow-up to "He's You All Over Again" was never far from her thoughts or anyone else's in the room. Then there was one more song, as Dusty had warned.

With the third song the mood changed yet again. It was a bona fide tearjerker called "Mama, I Want to Go with You." It told the story of a little girl's plea to go with her dying mother, just as the child had always gone everywhere with her.

"That's all I need to hear," Rhonda said halfway through the song. She quickly slid off the stool. "I've got to go. Carl's waiting. Big doings tonight. Right, guys? See you at the party before the show, I'm sure," she said and immediately left the room before anyone else could even move and without casting a glance in Dusty's direction.

Within seconds she was back down the hallway to where Carl was waiting patiently in a reception area. Without saying a word, he opened the door, along with the umbrella. They were leaving the studio parking lot before she said anything. "Carl, I'm going to skip the mall. Just take me home."

"That damn Dusty," she cursed to herself. Her mind raced as the car slowly made its way from Music Row through the rain-clogged traffic and back to the interstate. She wanted to scream, but held back. *That goddamned, thoughtless creep. How could that piece of shit do that to me? Today of all days. Today, when I need a boost, that son-of-a-bitch knocks me down by bringing up Mama. I should never have told him anything. Anything.*

Softly, quietly, she gave in, as she'd often done where her mother was concerned, and let herself cry. As hurt and angry as she was, she was aware she couldn't risk crying at home where Roger would instantly want to know what was wrong and would be dead certain it had something to do with Dusty Harmon. And once again Roger was right about Dusty, she reminded herself. But why would Dusty do what he did? Gazing out the car window at the rain, she was glad Carl was watching the traffic closely and wouldn't notice her tears.

Slowly, the hurt and the memories overcame her anger as she recalled her mother and all those years of growing up with the morning glories, red clay, and heartbreaks in Darden, Alabama.

CHAPTER 4

The gently rolling Alabama countryside with its brilliant red clay and towering stands of oaks and loblolly pines was often tranquil and uneventful. But that wasn't always the case, especially in the center of a state, defiantly billed as the "Heart of Dixie," and particularly in Crenshaw County during the upheaval of the 1940s.

In the 1940s, at frequent intervals during World War II, the Allies transported captured German military personnel to the United States and Canada and kept them in prisoner of war camps in remote rural sections of both countries. One such camp was opened in 1943 in Crenshaw County, located about halfway between Montgomery and the Florida state line on Highway 331.

Perched on top of the bluffs overlooking the Big Caney River right outside the small town of Darden, Alabama, the prisoner camp was nestled in a large stand of pines, many of which had been cleared for constructing the facility. The camp consisted of four one-level wooden barracks buildings, each housing a hundred German prisoners. Nearby was a large combination mess hall and recreation building, along with a barn for storing farm equipment, as well as two separate units for toilets and makeshift showers.

At the entrance to the camp sat an old white frame farm-house used as a combination guard station and office for the local officials in charge of the entire operation. The compound was heavily wooded, except for several of the approximately eighty acres that had been cleared for growing vegetables and a cotton cash crop. Enclosed behind a ten-foot wire fence topped by two electrified stands of barbed wire, the camp had only one entrance, which fronted Big Caney Road.

The townspeople of Darden had as little to do with the German prisoners as they possibly could. At best tolerating the camp's presence as their patriotic duty, Darden residents stayed away from that part of the river and generally avoided venturing that far down Big Caney Road. Aside from the accepted mood of the community, once a month the Ladies Wesley Guild of the First Methodist Church of Darden sent out to the camp cakes, cookies, and other homemade goods, along with jams and canned vegetables when fresh ones weren't in season, in hope that the same kindness was being shown to American prisoners of war in Europe.

"It's the least we can do for those boys out there. The war's that Hitler's fault, not theirs. My grandfather was from Germany, and he was nothing like Hitler, I can assure you," was typical of the sentiments frequently expressed, particularly among those Darden residents of German descent.

The guards at the camp were local citizens paid by the United States government, too old to serve in the war effort overseas, and lucky to have those jobs at home. The sheriff of Crenshaw County was officially in charge of the camp and filed monthly status reports with the War Department in Washington, D.C. Each report was given great attention by the sheriff who took pride in what he saw as his contribution to the war effort. Sheriff Will Creighton chose one prisoner to work with him and the other guards whenever needed around the camp office. The prisoner chosen, the only one who spoke any English, made the selection an easy matter.

"I can just tell by looking at that boy that he's not like the rest of the 'krauts.' More trustworthy. He looks at you when you're talking to him," Sheriff Creighton said. The prisoner's name was Helmut Helwig. His home was a small village outside Nuremberg. At age twenty-five he was six feet of Nordic perfection capped by a stock of straight, flaming red hair.

And he was, without a doubt, the best-looking man Emma Scoggins had ever seen in person.

Raised in the Crenshaw County Home for Children, a five-building orphanage built during the Reconstruction Era, and in her mind not unlike the prison camp in some ways, Emma felt somewhat sympathetic toward the German boys on the Big Caney. When Sheriff Creighton asked, she readily agreed to go out to the camp once a week to clean the guards' office and generally straighten up the rest of the old farmhouse, especially the kitchen, and particularly after a holiday when the sheriff treated the guards to a home-cooked lunch with all the trimmings.

Emma lived alone in a three-room apartment over the garage behind the First Methodist Church on Waterloo Street in downtown Darden. As payment for the apartment, she cleaned the church sanctuary, Sunday school classrooms, offices, and the parsonage next door, where Reverend Harlan T. White and his wife, Grace, lived with their two small daughters. Beginning each spring and lasting well into the fall, Emma also took care of the church's "victory garden." She was welcome to help herself from the neat rows of tomatoes, yellow squash, pole beans, yellow onions, white corn, and cucumbers being grown "for God's work" in the community and for church suppers every other Wednesday evening after prayer meetings.

At age sixteen Emma dropped out of Crenshaw County High School and immediately went to work cleaning the homes of her more well-to-do classmates. "I don't mind much. I'm at their houses during the day, and they're at school or off doing something most of the time," she said when the pastor's wife asked. She was a plain-looking girl with light brown wavy hair, a sallow complexion, and large green eyes. Because of her shyness, she had always been unfairly regarded as being slow in her mental development. She had a slight limp from an accident when she was eight. A local farmer had brought one of his ponies to the orphan-age so the children could ride one summer afternoon. Toward the end of the day, the spirited animal became tired and annoyed by the screaming children. Once Emma was in the saddle, she was immediately thrown and kicked by the contrary animal. Her left leg never healed correctly, but she always acted as if nothing was wrong. Even as a child Emma didn't like to make a fuss about anything or call attention to herself.

"We might as well let Emma leave school. Cleaning or field work is about all she'll likely ever be able to do," the school principal conceded, after two of Emma's teachers made the suggestion and the orphanage superintendent went along. Emma never actually knew whose idea it was in the first place, but asked no questions.

When she turned eighteen, Emma left the orphanage. She was allowed to find her own place to live with the bless-ing of the orphanage superintendent who needed her bed at the institution. When the former church minister's wife approached her, the job offer and accompanying place to live sounded perfect to her, and she had lived behind the church ever since.

It was 1944 and at age thirty-two Emma remained grateful for what she considered her good fortune at the church all those years. She truly enjoyed the nice people, hand-me-down clothes, and church supper leftovers that came her way. After dropping out of school, Emma had no real friends. Her social life was limited to trips to the market and brief conversations with people whose homes she cleaned. She spent her nights by herself in the apartment over the garage with her one luxury, a Philco radio she'd saved for several months to buy. She was always alone, except for her big yellow tom she named Rhett, a gift from the minister's wife. Emma's only regular extravagance was treating herself to a movie at the Princess Theatre, where she sat to one side in the back row. She saw *Gone with the Wind* three times when it finally made it to Darden and was all the talk in town.

So she welcomed the opportunity for a change of pace and had no reservations about helping out at the prisoners' camp when Sheriff Creighton asked her after the Methodist Ladies Wesley Guild recommended Emma for the job. "Emma's a good hard worker, Sheriff. And the girl has absolutely no interest in men," was part of the guild's endorsement. She had never had a date in her life. Once Tommy Hardin at the orphanage playfully dunked her while they were swimming in the Big Caney, but he had been whipped so hard for doing it he never again spoke to Emma, who hadn't minded what Tommy did. Emma didn't complain about anything, even in her most private thoughts.

Whenever Emma went to work at the prisoners' camp on Big Caney Road, she was driven by one of the church deacons, who delivered her and baked goods from the Ladies Wesley Guild at the same time. Later each day, almost always on a Monday, a guard leaving duty gave Emma a ride back to town about five miles away.

"Here, Helmut. Come on and help with these things in the car," the sheriff said as he watched the black Chevrolet drive up to the compound early one Monday morning. By the time the car was through the gate, leaving a cloud of red dust in its wake and parked by the front porch of the old farmhouse, Sheriff Creighton and his German office assistant were standing on the porch ready to unload the food from the church.

Emma sat on the backseat of the car holding a large tray of brownies covered with a white cloth. Woody Stewart drove the car that day and came around to shake hands with the sheriff who was opening the door for Emma.

"Morning, Bill," Stewart said to the sheriff.

"Good to see you, Woody," the sheriff replied. "You've got quite a load there, Emma. Here, I'll help with that one on top. Looks heavy."

"Bill, the rest of it's in the trunk. It's not locked," Stewart told him.

By that time Emma had stepped out of the car and was reaching into the backseat for more of the baked goods. Turning, she noticed the young German soldier for the first time. She merely nodded and let him take the cardboard box from her hands when he reached for it. Between them no words were spoken then or for the rest of that day as each went about their assigned chores.

Emma carefully rearranged the white cloth over the tray of brownies the sheriff was holding and immediately proceeded into the house to begin her weekly cleaning, leaving the men to talk and unload the rest of the things from the car. Throughout that Monday, Emma went about her usual activities and pretended she couldn't overhear anything said by the sheriff, the guards, or the handsome German prisoner. But from their conversations she came to realize the prisoner would be in the office often.

Back at home that evening, she confided to Rhett about how she felt. "Well, maybe not *better* looking than Errol Flynn or Douglas Fairbanks, Jr.," she said. "But just as good. And I don't have to pay ten cents to see *him*," she said. She was pleased knowing the next Monday was not far away.

When she returned to the camp the following week, Helmut met her at the car and opened the door, giving her much more attention than she was accustomed to having. That day she ate lunch on the front porch of the farmhouse, something she preferred to do when weather permitted. She had brought her favorite summertime sandwich of homemade mayonnaise and thick slices of tomato, along with a cold fried chicken leg from the night before. She felt disappointed as she watched the young German walk back to the mess hall to eat with the other prisoners. But when he returned more quickly than she expected, she was still sitting on the porch, her lunch bag neatly folded in her lap. He handed her a sugar cookie and said, "Too many for me." At that moment from inside the house, a voice called him, "Helmut, step on in here for a minute." That was the first time Emma had heard his name.

Mondays at the camp overlooking the Big Caney River became an eagerly anticipated event for Emma. Helmut had learned her name and pronounced it with a long "e." When he said her name, it was "EEEmma."

Once, he helped her pick up a stack of papers she had accidentally knocked off one of the two desks in the front room of the house. On another occasion she helped him hang a somber picture of President Roosevelt over the mantle. There were usually few words exchanged between them, mostly simple hand gestures, although Emma was confident she would understand every word Helmut might ever say to her.

At home at night she would laugh and tell Rhett how Helmut spoke. "Rhett, you should hear him talk. He calls me 'EEEmma,'" she mimicked, dragging out the "e." "It might sound funny around here in Darden, but he does really good," she bragged.

Weeks later Emma was once again sitting by herself on the house porch eating her lunch. Returning from his own meal with the other prisoners, for the first time Helmut smiled at Emma and sat down on the front steps rather than going into the house. Emma was sitting in a straight-back, cane-bottom chair a few feet from the steps. She started to offer him a piece of her special carrot cake when one of the guards summoned Helmut inside to help with moving a desk. Rising reluctantly, Helmut again smiled at his companion and looked back at her from the door. Her eyes followed him into the house. Somewhat embarrassed that he had seen her watching him, she quickly looked down at her clothes and smoothed her skirt over her legs.

Aware of her plain features, drab hair, and thick calves that left no hint of an ankle, Emma always made a special effort to look neat. Her few dresses, mostly hand-me-downs, were always ironed and starched to perfection. She mended her black cardigan sweater frequently, taking pains not to pucker the weave of the wool. If she had a feature she thought pretty, she fancied her large green eyes. Even without make-up, something she didn't own, her eyes stood out from her otherwise ordinary face.

By early fall, Emma and Helmut developed a quiet rapport, making each Monday the long anticipated part of an otherwise uneventful week for both of them. Glances, small courtesies, the accidental touching of hands while working together—each took on a special significance for the two of them.

It was an unusually warm late October afternoon. The camp guards were with all the other prisoners down at the river for a recreation break from the farm work. Sheriff Creighton had gone back to Darden unexpectedly to pick up a package at the post office and had seen no harm in leaving Emma and Helmut alone in the house, if he even gave it a thought. At first with gentle hesitation and then with great passion, the orphan cleaning woman and her handsome German idol made love.

At first, Emma was terrified to think she was pregnant. They had made love only once. But later she became defiant, even proud of her secret, her prize, as she thought of the baby she was carrying. Never a slim girl, she was able to hide the development of her pregnancy easily with full fitting dresses and aprons. Early on, she decided to wait to tell even Helmut. Wait for what she was not sure, but she felt it better to keep her secret to herself, at least until the right moment.

Early on Thursday afternoon May 8, 1945, Emma was startled by the church bells and the blasts from Darden's fire siren. The siren sounded longer than she could ever remember. But she continued cleaning the church sanctuary. Without ever inquiring about the siren, when she finished she immediately went back to her apartment over the garage, where she stayed until mid-afternoon on Saturday. She left a note on the door of the church parsonage telling the minister's wife she had slightly strained her back and needed to rest. She assured Mrs. White there was nothing to be concerned about. By Saturday afternoon, feeling somewhat better and less worried, Emma walked three blocks down Waterloo Street to McGee's Market to buy milk and some other items she needed.

Entering the grocery store, she was greeted by Mrs. McGee who was standing in her usual spot behind the cash register. "Emma, did you ever think in all your days we'd hear news like this? I mean this is wonderful," Mrs. McGee said as she struggled with both hands to stick a loose bobby pin back into her tightly wound bun.

Emma merely looked at the storeowner with a puzzled expression. She had no idea what the older woman meant about the "news."

"The war, Emma," Mrs. McGee stated. "Or I should say, the peace. Didn't you hear? The war's over in Europe. Those horrible Germans surrendered. Didn't you hear all the commotion on Thursday? Why, that siren rang until I thought it would explode."

Emma had no telephone and hadn't turned her radio on, preferring to sleep until she felt better. "No, Mrs. McGee. I've been home not feeling my best," Emma replied. "Of course, I'm happy," she added, and slowly turned away. She left the store without getting anything.

Outside the store Emma stopped and grasped a light pole with one hand, afraid she was going to be sick or possibly faint. She had never thought much about the war ending or what might happen to Helmut if it did, or even what would happen to her or their baby. Slowly, she walked back toward the church.

She saw Sheriff Creighton's car approaching.

She waved for him to stop, gathered her strength, and walked across the street to the sheriff's open car window.

Before she could say a word, the sheriff repeated the same sentiments expressed by Mrs. McGee. It was all anyone in Darden could talk about.

"Yes, I'm very happy," Emma managed to say weakly.

"Well, it looks like you'll have some spare time on Mondays for a change, Emma," the sheriff said. "But don't think for one minute we haven't appreciated all your help out there at the camp. But I can't say I'm very sorry to have all that behind us and finally over with."

"What do you mean, Sheriff?" she asked. "I'll be out on Monday as usual."

"No, no, no. No need for that anymore, Emma. All the prisoners were shipped out on the early train just before dawn this morning. They're going straight to Canada and then back home to Germany. Whatever's left of it."

CHAPTER 5

When Emma's little girl was born, no one asked who the father was or paid very much attention. After giving birth at the local hospital, Emma was allowed to use an extra room at the orphanage for a few days, rather than go home to her apartment and be alone. The Crenshaw County public health nurse looked in on her and the baby during the nurse's daily visits to tend on the children. And Emma felt at home there, as nowhere else. She had been raised at the orphanage since her own mother had died while giving birth to her. "It just seems right being here," she remarked to the nurse.

Emma's baby girl had bright red curly hair people at the orphanage described as "a sight to behold." Emma named her Rose. In her private thoughts Emma saw her precious baby girl as a reminder of the one cherished moment when nothing else had mattered, the only love she had truly ever known. And she was certain she would never be alone again.

In fact, being alone was practically impossible for Emma after Rosie, as she called her, arrived. Having no one to leave her with, Emma took Rosie everywhere she went. Whether cleaning the church, the parsonage, or other homes in Darden, she had the child right there with her. Rosie went from lying in a large wicker basket to toddling around wher-

ever her mother was working. By age four, Rosie sat dutifully in a chair and colored or played with her favorite rag
doll while Emma cleaned. Frequently, Rosie got to play with
the children who lived in the homes while her mother
worked. That routine continued until Rosie entered
Crenshaw County Elementary School where she did well
and was popular with the other children. Rosie's teachers
told Emma her little girl was very bright, and Emma constantly encouraged her. "Use your head, Rosie, and the sky's
the limit. You'll see. And don't let anyone ever tell you you
can't do something. If you can't or just plain don't want to,
that's for you to decide, not them," she told her.

For Rosie, school was a welcome change from watching
her mother clean toilets, mop floors, and wash fancy dishes.
But the daily respite lasted only from eight o'clock each
weekday morning until three, when the school bell rang and
she returned to the garage apartment.

In her sophomore year at Crenshaw County High
School, home of the Fighting Rebels, Rosie had an
announcement for her mother. "Mama, I'm going to try out
for the cheerleading squad. Everyone says I have a real good
chance. And I'll still keep up with my homework. I promise."
Rosie had developed into a tall, striking young girl with
scarlet hair, perfect skin, large green eyes, and a figure many
of the other girls envied.

Several days passed following Rosie's announcement, and
Emma thought little more about it. One Tuesday afternoon
in late August that changed. Emma was in the sanctuary of
the First Methodist Church putting a fresh coat of paste wax
on the aging, dark oak pews. It was unusual for anyone to
come into the church during that time of day, so Emma was
particularly startled when Mrs. Wesley Drake, the assistant

principal from the high school and a prominent member of the church, came in and asked Emma if they could talk for just a minute. Without asking, Emma dutifully sat down in the pew she was waxing, while her caller sat in the pew directly across the newly carpeted aisle that ran down the center of the room.

"Emma," Mrs. Drake began immediately, "I know nothing's ever been easy for you. You've worked hard so many years, and I would never want to add to any difficulties you might have. But I have been asked to talk to you about your Rosie."

"Has Rosie done something wrong, Mrs. Drake?"

"No, Emma, it's nothing like that. What I'm talking about is her going out for the cheerleading squad. We just don't think it sets a good example. Just isn't right. Her not having a father and being put out front as an example of the school's finest. Now there's nothing wrong with Rosie. She's wonderful. A good student, so pretty and high spirited. Her grades are excellent, you must know that. It's just all that other that makes us feel makes a difference. Do you know what I'm saying?"

Emma still sat without saying anything. Out of habit she took her cleaning cloth and started wiping the pew in front of her. "No, Mrs. Drake, maybe I'm not just getting what you mean. But I may have a good idea. I've always wanted what's best for Rosie. She deserves that and more, all children do for that matter. But there's one thing I've come to understand, and I suppose Rosie has a pretty good idea about it herself. It's that there're some things just can't be changed, some people who just won't be changed. You and others have always been kind to me. But it's the same kindness you might show a common dog." Emma kept waxing the pew. Then she continued. "There's a difference in kindnesses, Mrs. Drake. Some people never bother to figure that out. I just hope my Rosie learns the difference before it's too late for her."

Mrs. Drake started to reply, but Emma wasn't finished with what she had to say. "Yes, I guess I really do know what you're getting at. And I know you're probably doing what you think's best. But how can I expect my daughter to understand anything like what you're saying? She's just herself. She's not me. She's not Emma Scoggins. She's Rosie. She didn't do anything wrong. People may say I did, but why punish the child? It ain't right. Not fair at all."

"Well, fair . . ."

For the first time Emma looked across the aisle. "Mrs. Drake, my daughter didn't ask to be brought into this world. That's what I did. She hasn't asked for a better world. That's something I can only try to do. But if she deserves a world that's more fair, well, that's where people like you come in."

Mrs. Drake replied, "Well, Emma, you don't have to tell her what all I said. Make up something. Tell her you can't afford the cheerleading uniform. Surely you've had to tell her something like that before."

"Oh, yes, there've been those times," Emma replied. "That she'd understand all too well."

"No, Emma. You must speak to her. Tell her whatever you want, but that's the way it has to be. I'm sorry." Mrs. Drake quickly left the church, and Emma moved on to the next pew.

Later that evening when they talked, Rosie told her mother exactly how she felt. "I know what you're telling me, Mama. I understand. I really do. Honest. But I don't want you to worry about me either. It's the grown-ups, not my friends. For some reason grown-ups have funny ideas about things, a lot of things. But it doesn't bother me. Never has. You've always shown me it's best to just go along about your own business." Then she added, "And something else. I know there's a lot more to this world than Darden, Alabama. After I'm grown, I'm going to find out for myself. Sure, there's plenty of time before that. Guess I'll just have to spend it teasing Whacker Rawlins. That's always fun."

They both laughed. Emma was relieved, but had no idea why teasing the Rawlins boy might be fun or even why he was called that by his friends. "Mama, you and I have so much. More than so many of my friends do. Their parents fight all the time. Well, maybe not all the time, but a lot. But when I come home to our place," there was a slight catch in her throat, "well, you're here. And there's just so much that's good. I love you, Mama." Their hug lasted for several minutes as they both cried quietly, interrupted only by the aging Rhett's demand to be fed.

Rosie Scoggins graduated from Crenshaw County High School with fine grades and without ever being a cheerleader. In her senior year, her classmates elected her "Best Looking Girl." The mother of the "Best Looking Boy," Ronnie Rawlins, instructed him not to hold Rosie's hand in the yearbook photograph. However, that didn't bother Rosie. She had always thought Ronnie Rawlins, called "Whacker" by his male buddies because masturbating was his only known hobby, was "a pimpled, wavy-haired simpleton" as Rosie put it.

For the yearbook photograph with Ronnie Rawlins, Rosie wore a tight-fitting red dress she intentionally bought one size too small and had her flaming red hair in a Rita Hayworth mass of curls slightly over her left eye. It didn't matter to her that the picture was black and white. Rosie just wanted to look great, to give everyone, even simple Whacker, something to think about. And it worked very well.

Whether Whacker's mother ever asked him why he had insisted on holding a book over his crotch in the picture no one ever knew. Rosie and Whacker's buddies knew all too well the answer to that, which also explained the marvelous, wide grin on Rosie's beautiful face in the yearbook. For Rosie that picture was a triumph—small, but a triumph just the same.

CHAPTER 6

Within months after her daughter's graduation from high school, Emma was once again alone. Rosie pleaded with her mother, "Mama, I'll never be anything or anybody as long as I stay in Darden."

Emma more than understood.

"Mama, I can get a job in Montgomery and come home on weekends. I promise. Honest I will. Montgomery isn't far at all, and the bus runs regularly between here and there. I've already checked. Mama, I love you, but you've never been out of Darden in your whole life. I can't be like that. I want more than that. I want to see some things, some of those things we read about in school," she said. "I know it'll be hard for a while on both of us. But I'll be coming in the door so often you won't think I'm even gone. I promise."

True to her word, Rosie returned to Darden almost every weekend with stories about her job and her new friends in the Alabama capital. Later, however, when she changed jobs after a few months as a sales clerk at the Parks-Belk department store, she decided not to tell Emma.

In her new job Rosie worked as a cocktail waitress in a popular bar in downtown Montgomery near the business district and the capitol building with its gold dome. The pay was much better, and the tips made a big difference. When she could, she took her mother a blouse or something else in a Parks-Belk box. Emma always made a fuss and said Rosie shouldn't have spent her money that way, even though her mother cherished each gift and loved to show them off to the minister's wife as often as she could.

"You were right, Rosie," Emma finally admitted during one of Rosie's visits. "Montgomery is better for you than Darden ever would be. But don't forget where home is."

A little more than two years later, Emma was working in the church garden late one June afternoon. When Reverend White's wife, Grace, walked over to check on the tomatoes and pole beans, Emma was eager to share her news. "My Rosie got married last week," she proudly announced.

"Why, Emma, you don't say," Mrs. White squealed. Grace White was well known for always making an effort to sound positive and perky about everything, except for death, though she said even death could be a blessing. Once she was in the First National Bank of Darden, when she overheard an elderly farmer at the next teller's window say, "It always seems as if I'm having to borrow from Peter to pay Paul." At that point, eager to find something positive to say, the reverend's wife loudly interjected, "But aren't you glad you've got a Peter!" The startled farmer slowly nodded affirmatively as everyone in the bank who had heard her remark, but nothing the farmer had first said, turned to stare at her. Red-faced, Grace White fled the bank without ever making her deposit.

"Yes, Rosie called and caught me in the church office and told me this morning. She and her husband are coming to see me this weekend if he can get off from work. He's a salesman, Rosie said. He sells carpet and vacuum cleaners all over southern Alabama," Emma explained.

"Well, Emma, that sounds truly wonderful," Grace White said. "I know you're just thrilled. Rosie's such a beautiful girl, and I'm just certain she married a real prince. Be sure to have them say hello while they're here. Such a beautiful girl. He's a real lucky man. I just hope he realizes how really lucky he is," Mrs. White said, giving Emma a quick hug and almost dropping the basket of tomatoes she had picked.

But just as Rosie never told her mother about her job in the bar, she made sure Emma never found out her husband frequently came home drunk, and all too often used his fist to make any point he felt needed emphasizing. The southern charmer she dated for months turned into a nightmare within weeks of their marriage.

"Beats the holy shit out of you," was how Rosie's waitress friend put it. "No way I'd take that kinda crap off no man, honey. Life's too damned short to spend it black and blue from some redneck who can't hold his liquor."

On those evenings Terry Haynes came home and went into a rage over the slightest thing he found that didn't please him. Once she could get away from him, Rosie would run out the back door of the one-bedroom frame home they rented and quietly slip back in the door to the screened porch on the front of the house. There she would sleep on a metal glider until she knew her husband had passed out in the bedroom. She kept a green and white afghan her mother had crocheted over one arm of the glider for just such occasions, in case the night turned cool.

A virgin when she met Terry, Rosie's first experiences with sex went from playful to rough after the marriage. With all the class of a rutting pig, Terry Haynes began forcing himself on his wife with his stale breath and sweat laced with the smell of too much beer. Months into the marriage nothing changed. "I don't understand why a man making love has to curse you," she finally confided to her closest friend at work.

Having been married three times, Rosie's listener had a ready answer. "Sounds to me like old Terry's trying to over-come a small cock problem. He's like a lot of men who use alcohol to convince themselves they've got what it takes. It's the lack of equipment—that's what's really bothering the bastards. It's not anything you're doing, honey. Not one bit. Hell, I had the same thing happen with this guy named Stan I used to date. It was before I married my second husband. You see, Stan was always trying to hit a home run with a Popsicle stick. He finally got the message one night when I yelled, 'Batter up, three strikes and no balls' and walked out. Never saw that jerk or his Popsicle stick again after that. Guess Stan decided to try and charm some other fool with his 'technique' as he called it."

But Rosie feared her husband's problem went far beyond the size of anything. After each humiliating sexual encounter, she retreated to her side of the bed and waited for his heavy snoring to signal it was safe for her to get up. Since their place wasn't air-conditioned and Terry insisted on keeping the electric fan directed toward his side of the bed, the only way Rosie could escape his clammy stench and find a cool, safe place to hide was to seek refuge in the kitchen or on the porch.

The abuse and Rosie's initial feelings of helplessness last-ed for more than a year. But Emma never knew anything that happened. Rosie was determined to handle the situation herself, although the incidents became more violent and the bruises harder to cover with make-up or long sleeves. She and Terry visited Emma only three times after their marriage, but Rosie called her mother at the church at least once a week to check on her and to make excuses about why they couldn't come to Darden.

Terry tossed an empty can into the water and told Rosie to hand him another Pabst.

"How many we got left?" he asked.

Rosie looked into the cooler in the bottom of the boat. "There's a few more, and they'll just have to do you," she replied. "No sense in going all the way back to the dock this late, just for more beer."

"I didn't ask your damned opinion, Rosie. What I asked was how many beers are in the damned cooler."

"Four," she replied without having to check again. She and her husband were in a small aluminum fishing boat in the middle of Lake Hood, a few miles north of Montgomery. In the spring and summer months particularly, Terry often fished in the evenings after work, when hungry catfish were especially easy to catch. It was a hot, humid night in early August. Rosie accepted one of his rare invitations to go along with him to escape the heat of the house and, she hoped, to keep him from getting too drunk.

"Rosie, honey, I'll decide if four beers is enough or not and when we need to go back," he stated. "Why in the hell-I'd you come out here if all you're gonna to do is bitch?"

When she heard the word "bitch" come out of his mouth, a cold chill went through her entire body. Each time he beat her he used the word over and over as he hit her. "You bitch! I'll teach you, bitch!" he would shout.

"Terry, I'm not complaining about anything and you know it," she replied. "I just said you've got enough beer to last, that's all. Looks to me like you've got your hands full catching all those fish to fool with much else."

Terry hadn't heard a word she said. "Well, Miss Know-it-all, if you can't do what I ask, why don't you just get out and go home right now? And don't worry about swimming. Just walk across the damned water like that mother of yours must have taught you living in that fucking church."

To Rosie, abuse was one thing. Talking badly about her mother was quite another. "I'm sure she taught me a hell of a lot more than anyone ever taught you, unless it was how not to drink. And you must have learned that somewhere all too well."

The next few moments happened so fast she had to think hard to recall them later. Terry held his fishing rod in his left hand and swung his right fist at his wife. Ducking his fist, Rosie crouched down, holding on to one side of the boat with both hands as the blow missed. Then, throwing his rod into the bottom of the boat, all six feet of Terry Haynes stood up and stepped toward her.

"You fucking bitch. I'll teach you a thing or two myself."

He lunged toward her. The boat rolled over, throwing both of them into the dark water.

Rosie held on to the capsized boat with one hand and struggled to remove her canvas shoes with the other. Several feet away Terry surfaced, thrashing about with both arms as he coughed and gasped for air. The light of the moon was almost totally blocked by clouds. All she could see was the white foamy bubbles he was making with his frantic actions.

"Rosie, I can't swim!" he bellowed and again disappeared beneath the surface of the water, then immediately reappeared, struggling even more violently.

She was amazed at what she heard and saw.

"Help me! Give me a hand!" he gasped and again sunk beneath the water.

Only a split second passed before she made up her mind. Rosie slowly pushed the boat away, still holding on. She never looked back. The noise of his gurgling and muffled shouts lasted only a few seconds longer. Then her nightmare was over. That night Terry Haynes' abuse ended in the dark waters of a peaceful lake.

Rosie pushed the boat to shore and walked until she was found by another fisherman, who contacted the Highway Patrol office in Montgomery. Later that night she was driven back home, where a State Trooper stayed on the front porch to make sure she was all right. The trooper stayed at Rosie's until a friend she had called arrived and brought back the Plymouth Savoy she had left at the dock. Rosie never wanted to see the boat again and sent word to the dock manager to sell it for whatever he could get. She told him to keep half for himself for his trouble. The next afternoon the Alabama Wild Game authorities found her husband's body near the Lake Hood dam, where it finally surfaced.

Because of a really bad cold and high fever, Emma wasn't able to attend her son-in-law's funeral in Cullman. "It's all right, Mama. Funerals are hard, and it's all the way over in Okalatchee County anyway. I'll be all right, honest," Rosie assured her.

After the funeral, Rosie immediately went back to Darden, but only to visit. She wanted to tell Emma what she had decided to do. "Mama, there're too many unhappy memories in Montgomery for me now. And you know I can't come back here to Darden. What could I do here?" she began.

"Rosie, I've always known you to know what's best for

you," Emma replied. "Do you have something you really want to do?"

"No particular thing as such," she responded. "But I want to find a job somewhere else. I've been thinking about going to Nashville, if I can. Ava Dale, my old roommate before I married Terry, has been living in Nashville ever since I married. She called right after she heard about Terry and said I could move in with her anytime I want. She's married now and has a kid, but it would be a real help for a little while, until I could get a place of my own."

"Nashville seems awfully far," Emma said.

"Not really, Mama. And Tennessee's just got to be a whole lot like Alabama. Ava Dale says Nashville's a great place. She loves the music and I do, too. And it's the state capital, same as Montgomery. Has to be the same sort of people there." On late nights Rosie and her friend, Ava Dale Walters, had spent hours singing along with the jukebox at the bar where they both worked. The jukebox had nothing but country songs on it, and the regulars said the girls sounded pretty good, especially on the slow tunes with harmony. Rosie had a favorite Patsy Cline song she especially loved to perform.

"Maybe you're right, Rosie. Tennessee can't be too different. And besides, whatever they've got going great there, you'll find it. Surely better luck than Montgomery or Darden." Emma paused. She took a deep breath, her thoughts never far from the past. "You've been through a lot, learned a whole lot of things the hard way. But you've survived. Still have a spirit that's a real blessing. Do what you want, Rosie. Your mama's sure you're right. Just don't forget where home is."

CHAPTER 7

"Ava Dale, that bathtub has more rings than the planet Saturn." Rosie and Ava Dale Walters were standing in the only bathroom in the Walters' house in east Nashville.

"Oh, I know, I know," Ava Dale apologized. "I did manage to clear off some room on this shelf for your personal things. But little Michelle just wouldn't take her nap this morning. She flat refused and that pretty much kept me chasing after her all day. But she should conk out early tonight, so I can get something done around this place."

"I'm only teasing, Ava Dale." Rosie grinned and gave her hostess another hug. "Believe me, I know how hard it is to try and keep house while you do other things, too." She began to take her cosmetics out of a small bag and place them carefully on the shelf. "This will be fine."

"Mitch gets up real early and goes to work, so the bathroom shouldn't be a problem after he's gone." Ava Dale's three-year-old daughter had left the room, no longer intrigued with Rosie, who had arrived only moments earlier after driving from Montgomery to Nashville. "I've got to find Michelle. Why don't you go on in the living room when you're through in here? I'm sure there's at least two or three beers left from last night. Mitch promised he'd bring home some more after work tonight. I'll get Michelle and the beer. Then you can catch me up on all the dirt. And we can talk about all the crazy things we did in Montgomery. I still haven't told Mitch everything. Probably never will, if I stay smart. And you've got to tell me all about your plans."

The only problem, Rosie had to acknowledge, was that she had no plans she knew of, at least nothing very definite. She was convinced she wanted no part of another clerking job in some huge department store. She was equally determined not to become a glorified coffee maker in some office, particularly at a bank. She told herself she would hold out for something better, more interesting. Hold out as long, at least, as she could tolerate her friend's two-bedroom combination toy store and laundry. Toys were strewn everywhere; the laundry was hung all over the kitchen and bath.

When Ava Dale wasn't complaining about her husband's snoring, attempting potty training, or screaming at Michelle and apologizing profusely for doing so each time, she was talking about country music. And that was just fine with Rosie. Driving her faded, two-tone blue Plymouth Savoy to Nashville, Rosie switched from one country radio station to another as soon as the static got louder than the music. By the time she reached Ava Dale's, she was thinking very seriously about trying to get some kind of work in the music business. She didn't know exactly what at that point, but she was certain she would find out. Recalling her mother's prediction that Rosie would be lucky in Nashville, she promised herself she would prove Emma was right.

Three weeks passed. The job-hunting in Nashville hadn't been as easy as Rosie had assumed from Ava Dale's bragging about the city. Job interviews were mostly for the kind of dead-end jobs Rosie had vowed to avoid if at all possible, so she was still living with the Walters. She stayed away from the Walters' house as much as she could, partly to give Ava Dale and Mitch some privacy. "Ava Dale, this is Mitch's house, too, and, if he wants to spend two hours in the bathroom reading, that's his privilege. Honest, I don't mind waiting. I've always got an extra Kotex in my purse if things get too bad."

Eventually, Rosie found out about a job. "It's perfect. At least a start in the direction I've been looking for," she told Ava Dale. "If you all can put up with me for maybe one more week, two at the most, I can get my own place and leave you alone. You've been so good to me. I can never pay you back."

"Rosie Scoggins Haynes, I'll make you think 'move out,'" Ava Dale protested. "You're family and you'll stay as long as you can stand it. But I want to hear all about the job. Where's it at?"

Rosie then explained about the opening for a waitress at the Blue Note Lounge, a well-known nightspot on Broadway in downtown Nashville. "It's just a block from the Ryman Auditorium where the Opry is and—"

"Oh, I know all about the Blue Note, at least by reputation," Ava Dale assured her. "I've never been, but that's where all the stars and big shots go after the Grand Ole Opry every Saturday night. There's always live music and sometimes even the big stars get up and sing with the ones trying to get discovered down there. I hear they're all just like one big family."

"I know it's just waiting tables. Just beer, you understand. But at least I won't be stuck behind some teller's cage counting other people's money. If anyone brings something stronger to drink, they brown bag it, and that's okay with the owners."

"There's no telling who you'll meet down there, Rosie,"

Ava Dale continued on her trip through the galaxies of country music. "And God, honey, with your looks, you'll be a big hit in a place like that. You were made for it," she gushed. "You just have got to swear you'll tell me everything, and I do mean every little thing. You are so lucky. I could just spit fire and cry all at the same time!"

Rosie had to laugh at her friend's excitement. "I promise to spare no details about anything. If some fool spills a beer on me, you'll know the brand and where I kicked him." Ava Dale screamed with laughter. "And the first time a star makes a pass at me, I'll tell him I have to tell you everything and that's just all there is to it." They both hugged tightly and shook each other.

All along, Rosie had a good feeling that Nashville had been the right move for her. Besides, she liked to remind herself, Emma had said so, and Rosie always valued her mother's wisdom about life and the ways of the world, even as limited as Emma's world was, a world that had never been as kind as Rosie knew Emma deserved.

"Hey, Red, the guys need a girl singer tonight. Bonnie, their regular gal's done run off to Waco with that Texan's been hanging around her trailer. They need someone, a female, to sing with Arnold. Just harmony and backup for a couple of sets, until they can get a regular. If you're interested, why don't you go on over there? Arnold's sitting right over there." Mike Knight, the manager of the Blue Note Lounge, also originally from Alabama, had been impressed with Rosie from the beginning. "See if he's interested. I've heard you singing around here. You ought to be able to handle it. Heck, won't make much difference anyway, even if you don't know all the words just yet. As good as you look, your singing won't matter," he said and winked. "Heck, us red clay critters have to stick together in a pinch."

Originally from Waycross, Georgia, the "guys" to whom he referred billed themselves as the Webster Brothers. Their female singer had abruptly deserted them in the middle of their singing engagement at the Blue Note. Rosie's work hours were from noon until nine o'clock on weeknights and until midnight on Saturdays. She knew she could sing with the Webster Brothers after nine o'clock without cutting into her badly needed tip money. Determined to escape living with the Walters, she saved every dime she could.

Her singing arrangement with the Webster Brothers had worked well for Rosie and everyone else for a little more than two weeks, until one night Arnold Sands, the group's lead singer, suggested Rosie try a solo number. She was hesitant at first, but practiced in her car driving back and forth to work. After a few days she took him up on his offer. She chose one of the Webster Brothers' own songs, one she was particularly fond of entitled "Don't You Think It's Time." Feeling she might need the first set just to get her nerves settled, she insisted on performing only during the second set. That was one Friday night when she assured Arnold Sands, "I'm just one big nerve, but I'll try not to embarrass either of us."

The Blue Note Lounge was almost full the evening Rosie finally performed. It was two hours before midnight when "Darden, Alabama's own Rosie Haynes" was introduced by name for the first time to an audience of beer drinking music lovers in Music City USA. She wore a calico blouse borrowed from Ava Dale, who was sick and couldn't be there, and a dark blue skirt down to her ankles. With her shoulder length hair ablaze, she stepped up to the microphone and without any noticeable hesitation put her pounding heart into "Don't You Think It's Time." Anyone within listening distance agreed it was just that. Indeed, it was Rosie Haynes' time, and with it arrived Al Wendell.

Sitting with his wife to the left of the small stage about midway in the room, Al Wendell took one look at the new female singer and couldn't look at anything else. He recognized Rosie had the quality that separated the real class acts from all the others. It was unmistakable to him that she had presence, a crucial commodity for any entertainer. He told his wife beside him the singer had "a damn good natural voice, somewhat untrained, but with a terrific range." And she had the reddest hair Al Wendell had ever encountered, a hard red with the finest copper highlights. He prided himself in knowing a winner when he saw one, and there was no mistaking the fact there definitely was one that night at the Blue Note Lounge. Without hesitation, Al Wendell decided to cast his net in Rosie's direction.

Al Wendell hadn't always been a winner, by any means. In fact, he was a certified loser in many ways for many years. The Arkansas parole board knew Al Wendell as Paul Stinson, a small-time gambler who had served time for white slavery until he managed to escape from a roadside work detail with the assistance of a guard. He wasn't heard of again until federal agents caught up with him ten years later in Nashville. He had reinvented himself and managed to escape his entire past, including three ex-wives. In the early 1950s he maneuvered himself into the music business, an entire community in which the smooth-talking con artist found many to be on the take.

As Al Wendell, he fit right in and knew the music business would appreciate his talents. When the federal authorities finally found him, his clean record since his escape and the endorsement of not just a few prominent members of the music community helped him remain a free man, although on probation, which no one ever mentioned.

After eleven years hustling wide-eyed country music wannabes, that evening at the Blue Note Lounge Al Wendell hoped he was watching the latest, and, if he worked it right, as he characterized it to his wife, "the brightest light in my management career."

"Rosie, meet Al Wendell," her boss said as he introduced her to the heavyset balding man who had asked to meet her after the final set that evening. "Rosie, Al's quite a figure in this town. Some would say one of the best," he said as Wendell stood up and offered his hand, diamond rings and all.

"Please join us," Wendell said and indicated a chair. "This is my wife, Dawn."

Dawn Wendell smiled as she took Rosie's hand from her husband's grasp. "I really loved your song. Please sit here," she insisted, patting the empty chair next to hers rather than the one nearer her husband.

Rosie had to mentally pinch herself. She was finally sitting across from a Nashville bigwig, at least that was what her boss had said. She didn't know what to expect next, but knew she was willing to listen to the Devil himself to find out. In a flashback Rosie remembered how Ava Dale had warned her, "Listen, honey, you can always politely say no to anything you don't feel right about, but it don't cost nothing to just listen." *Ava Dale will not believe this,* she thought as she smiled at the Wendells.

Over the next hour Wendell explained who he was and what he did for up-and-coming artists. When Rosie first heard the word "artist," she was thrilled. According to

Wendell, he discovered new talent, found that talent the right material, hired a studio, and made a demonstration tape of a couple of songs he then took to record producers. "And I know them all," he assured her. "I also arrange singing engagements throughout the area to provide additional exposure," he further explained. He quickly asked Rosie if she would be interested in his services and handed her his business card.

Just as quickly she asked, "What will those services cost? I'm new here in Nashville, Mr. Wendell. This is my first and only job."

"You mean this is your first entertainment job any-where?" he asked.

"Oh no," she lied, "I've sung before, but this is my first singing work here. What I mean is this is the only paying job I have right now."

"I see. And your finances are pretty tight right now, I imagine. Could your family help you with expenses? At least for a while?"

"No, there's only my mother, and she can't help. But why should she?" Rosie replied. "I plan to pay for whatever I need, Mr. Wendell. I always have."

"No, my dear. No reason at all. It's just that you are prob-ably living on every dime you make here, unless I'm mistak-en. Beginning a fresh singing career will require other funds, as surely you might expect. I was merely asking about what resources you might have available. Just to give me an idea of what all I might need to arrange. That's really all I meant."

"My, yes, Miss Haynes, Al knows everyone and every-thing there is to know about this business. He just has to ask certain questions, you understand. For your benefit," Dawn Wendell chimed in.

Immediately, Rosie became apologetic. "I'm sorry, Mr. Wendell. Really I am. It's just—"

"No apology necessary, Miss Haynes. Can we talk further about this sometime? And it's Al to you."

"Please go ahead, Al. And I'm Rosie to both of you. You have to understand talking money has always made me antsy. I'm definitely interested. I assure you I really am."

Taking his cue, Wendell immediately made suggestions. "I want to start managing what I see can be a fine career for you. And I don't want you worrying about money all the time." He leaned forward and took his wife's hand on the table. "So why don't you move into our home, at least until you can get on your feet and all?"

"That sounds wonderful," Dawn agreed. "You wouldn't be the first of Al's clients to live with us for just the same reason, for just a little while at first. Besides, we have plenty of room. Our home's located in Hendersonville, just north of Nashville. A lot of the big stars have homes there on the lake. We have four bedrooms and three baths and a half. You'd have your own room, bath, and even a private entrance," she elaborated. "And our ten year old, Tony, will not be a problem. Why you're such a pretty thing, he'll probably just stare at you. He won't be in the way, I swear. And Rita, she's four, she just lives in front of our new television set, even when there's nothing on. That's her favorite play spot. She loves Milton Berle. Can't stand Sid Caesar, but I think you have to be older to appreciate him and that darling Imogene Coca, don't you? She's so zany. Imogene, not Rita," she said and laughed.

Then there was one more item Wendell wanted to discuss. "Are you using your real name?"

"Rosie Haynes is my real name, my legal name, if that's

what you mean." She preferred not to mention her maiden name or even that she had been married.

"I like the Haynes part," he began, "but you might want to consider changing your first name for professional reasons. Rosie sounds a bit cute for someone with your looks. Is there any name you're particularly fond of?"

The whole idea was out of the blue for Rosie. "I know entertainers change their names all the time, but I haven't ever thought about such a thing. I've only been doing this regularly for two weeks."

"You know what I think?" Wendell said. "Your red hair is tremendous. It hasn't hurt Rhonda Fleming any, either," he observed. Pausing briefly, he went on, "How does that sound to you? Rhonda Haynes. What do you think?"

Rosie's mind was flooded with all he had been saying. *Only moments ago I was singing a song, now he wants to change my name,* she thought. "That sounds fine, but I'd kind of like to think about it, if I could. You know. Write it down a few times to see how it looks. Say it in front of a mirror and that kind of thing. It sounds fine, but I do want to think about it."

Addressing her husband, Dawn Wendell said, "But, Al, so many lately are using double names. Don't you think she would need a middle name? And you know what? If I ever had another little girl, I'd name her Darlene. I just love the name Darlene." Quickly taking a sip of her gin and tonic, she continued before anyone could interrupt. "We can't have any more children," Dawn explained to Rosie, "but that's what I would do if we could and it was a girl. I had complications when Rita was born. There's a real cute Mouseketeer named Darlene, but you're a whole lot prettier, I think."

All the way home that night, Rosie sang "Don't You Think It's Time" and smiled at the strangeness of it all. She couldn't wait to tell Ava Dale everything. She knew her friend would undoubtedly want her to repeat it all a dozen times just to hear it over and over. While Ava Dale might find it hard to believe, it was all very real for Rosie. In her mind and out loud, she repeated, "Rhonda Haynes, Rhonda Haynes, Rhonda Haynes." She couldn't help but wonder what was next.

CHAPTER 8

The loud clank of metal garbage cans being tossed by trash collectors reminded Rhonda it was Thursday morning. She instantly sat up in bed, remembering she had an important appointment later that afternoon. Days before she had come to the conclusion she had to get away from the Wendells, all of them, and had taken the first step to accomplishing just that. On the day of her appointment, Rhonda wanted to get out of the Wendell house earlier than usual, before Al entangled her in one of his "surefire" ideas, which usually produced about as much heat as the broken lighter in her aged Plymouth.

Although she had to acknowledge the Wendell's hospitality over the past several months, letting her live in their house until she got a "real" contract with a record company, something Al assured her was bound to happen any day, the hospitality had its price. It hadn't taken Dawn Wendell long to start making other suggestions, particularly about Rhonda's hair.

"Have you ever considered toning it down some, honey? It's so bright red it probably stops traffic downtown," Dawn said.

And Tony Wendell's bursting in on her while she was in the bathroom, not once but four times, had taken its toll on Rhonda's nerves. Despite the boy's protests—"Honest, Miss Rhonda, I thought you were my sister in there"—she had long been on to the fact that the younger Wendell's initial awe had turned to simple, clumsy lust, even at his age. "I know very well," she told Ava Dale, "that if I bother to check I will find both pairs of my missing panties in his room somewhere, probably under the mattress or somewhere equally handy, probably for show and tell when his creepy friend, Ricky, comes over."

Aside from the many irritating things about the Wendell household, even more startling were the revelations about Al Wendell himself. Rhonda had been living with her agent's family for about seven months and working the gigs he had arranged when Scott Satterfield, a young street-smart free-lance talent scout who regularly covered all the entertainment bars in Nashville, suggested Rhonda join him for a drink without Wendell, who kept a tight rein on his number one find. Rhonda was aware of Satterfield's reputation for being honest and a skilled judge of what it took to make it in the music business.

"Ava Dale, this might be the chance I've been hoping for. To get out of the Wendell house for God's sake, and maybe get someplace on Music Row," she said to her friend when she told her about the telephone call.

Scott Satterfield had chosen the Hermitage Hotel as the site for his meeting with Rhonda. Named after President Andrew Jackson's famous home outside Nashville, the historic hotel had been the location for many political and business milestones in Nashville. Satterfield hoped his mid-afternoon rendezvous with Rhonda Haynes might be another.

When Rhonda arrived at the hotel a little past two in the

afternoon, her host was already seated in the ornate pillared bar downstairs next to the dining room. She soon realized Scott Satterfield had been there long enough to down a hefty portion of the bar's supply of Jack Daniel's.

"Sorry, Scott," Rhonda said, taking a seat next to Satterfield and thanking the young waiter who helped her with the chair.

"No problem. I'm here often enough that I haven't been too neglected," Satterfield said. "Anyway, it's already been a long day. Mine started at five o'clock, so I needed to unwind a little bit. Thanks for being here."

"I know what you're talking about," she replied as the waiter in the standard white coat arrived to take her drink order. "I'll have a bourbon and spring water." Rhonda had heard the term "spring water" used many times since coming to Nashville and used it whenever she wanted to impress someone.

"And I'll have another Jack in the Black over crushed ice," Satterfield said and handed his empty glass to the waiter.

When the waiter left the table, Satterfield turned to his guest and went straight to the point. "Rhonda, certain people in the business have taken notice of you. And they're quite impressed with what they see and hear. You've made an unusually hard luck job look practically easy. At least for you, that is," he began as he looked directly into her green eyes, which were fixed on him. "But I know I don't have to flatter you, either. You must know you're good. Damn good. Frankly, I'm curious about how you see your future, if I may ask?"

"Scott, I've been asked that more than once. Quite honestly, on one hand I think I know, but then, on one hand, I'm not so sure. If that makes sense. Especially if you consider some of the low life characters who've been doing the asking. Sure, I'm sort of doing what I want to do. But I'm not really sure about how it's going to work out, much less when. Al's doing a lot, all he can," she said half-heartedly, "but I don't know where it's all going and all that."

"Well, that's why I called you. Why I asked you to meet me for this drink today. To talk about Al himself and, most importantly, about you and your future, first and foremost."

After the waiter placed their drinks on the table, Satterfield continued. "How well do you know Al Wendell? What do you know about him?"

Before she could respond, he offered what he was almost certain she did not know about her agent. "The hard fact is that Al Wendell was in prison in Arkansas for white slavery. He disappeared and came to Nashville, changed his name and probably a lot of other things, but not enough in my opinion. He was clever enough to pick up on the sleazy con game some people run in the music business and even developed something of a knack in recognizing talent when he sees it."

Watching Rhonda slowly sip her drink and seeing her look of disbelief, he went on with the story. "Wendell's not a total fool by any means, but nor is he totally honest. Al finds talent or, even more often, a no-talent and sells himself as the man who can make it all happen. For a price, that is. And sometimes it's quite a price. Wendell arranges things like a demo tape, telling his clients he will play the tape for all the right publishing houses and producers and then continues to milk the unsuspecting future star for all they may be worth. And not just the so-called talent. Hell, he hits on the families. I know of one kid whose father was convinced by Wendell to mortgage the family farm in Oklahoma to finance Wendell and what he was supposed to do for the kid. Eventually, the kid had to go home to the farm, but there was nothing left at home. They lost it all to the bank. Everything was done under a stupid contract the kid and the kid's old man signed with Wendell. There was nothing anybody could do about it. And that's just one of several examples I could give you." He paused and took a long swallow of his bourbon.

Rhonda only stared at her drink. She had indeed signed a contract with Wendell within days of moving into the spare bedroom at the Wendell home. She suddenly felt sick to her stomach. She still had not responded to anything she had heard.

"You have a contract with Wendell, don't you?" Satterfield asked.

"Yes," she quietly replied, and took a long sip of bourbon and spring water.

Sensing her discomfort, he changed direction slightly. "Rhonda, you've got one great voice. I've seen you take a song and truly make it your own. I've heard you do it more than once. But there's more to it than that. A whole lot more, believe me. And I want you to listen carefully. When you're on that stage, you're the only one in anyone's mind. You flat take hold of an audience and then hold them in the palm of your hand. I've been there and seen it happen. And so have others around here. Important people. What you have is called presence. And only the truly great ones have it. They walk into a room, enter any conversation, and it belongs to them. They're born with it. Other people couldn't buy it if they fucking tried. Pardon my French."

"No problem," she said. "I'm just listening. And learning."

"If you were to have an opportunity to do better with your career, would you be interested?" he inquired.

Without telling Satterfield about all the boring gigs her

agent had arranged or Tony Wendell's raids on her underwear drawer and his sudden appearances when she was in the bathroom, she responded, "Sure, Scott. That goes without saying. I'd like to see what's out there for me. I've only been at this a short time, but I know there has to be something more than what Al's shown me."

"Now there's a real understatement. Of course there is." He leaned forward and placed both elbows on the table and folded his hands. "Do you have a copy of your contract with Wendell? At home, I mean." Before she could answer he said, "Never mind. I know what's in it without seeing it. They're all the same. Standard operation. The first thing is to get you out of that contract and that takes one thing—money. Could you or someone else help with a few bucks, if worse comes to worse?"

"No, there's just me. But I have managed to save a little. Living at the Wendell's rent free did have that one advantage."

"You know any decisions made have to be yours, but there are some alternatives. I can only tell you about them. Anything you do is your decision, but I can't help but think that it's in your best interest to get some more advice." He added, "Al Wendell never really expects to do anything big or worthwhile with anyone. He can't and knows it. The best he can do for himself, and he's the only person he's looking after, is to get someone under a contract and have someone else buy it out. That's his whole game. In the meanwhile he plays big shot and supports himself with the demo tape drain he runs on every naïve singer, picker, and their families he can get his hands on."

Rhonda was more than convinced and wanted to hear more. She finally smiled and asked, "Well, Mr. Know-it-all, what are you suggesting? Go ahead. Tell me."

Within a few days of their meeting, Scott Satterfield called Rhonda again. He actually called Ava Dale, as Rhonda had suggested, and asked her to have Rhonda call him. He did not want to risk tipping off Al Wendell. When they talked, Satterfield told Rhonda he had arranged for her to meet with Chuck Kaiser, the president of Sun Spot Records and one of the biggest movers and shakers on Music Row. Chuck Kaiser was well connected in Nashville's business community, something unusual for a recording executive in the early 1960s. Most others hadn't yet been accepted in the inner reaches of Nashville's old money business circles. But in Chuck Kaiser's case, it was a different story. He had someone on the inside of many enterprises, and they scratched each other's backs whenever necessary, quite often and always to their mutual benefit.

CHAPTER 9

Rhonda was careful not to give any hint to the Wendells about what might happen, and they seemed to suspect nothing. She hadn't even told Ava Dale. After her meeting at the hotel and the subsequent telephone conversation with Scott Satterfield, Rhonda kept her arranged appointment schedule in anticipation of the meeting with Chuck Kaiser, who was the acknowledged lord of Sun Spot Records, a major label in country music since the early fifties. It was a record label she had heard of dozens of times since coming to Nashville, and even had noticed on the jukebox back in Montgomery.

In many minds in the Nashville establishment, Chuck Kaiser represented the increasing, somewhat arrogant presence of outside money in the country music world. Handpicked by Sun Spot's parent Avanti Records in New York, Kaiser had moved into the Nashville scene from Ohio, where he had run a mid-sized manufacturing company with a management style his employees found reminiscent of the Spanish Inquisition. His New York bosses knew his reputation and sought him out through a headhunter, wanting Kaiser to establish a firmer grip on the country music segment of Avanti's corporate holdings.

"Chuck, with your legal background, we expect you to show those bumpkins a few things. For one, the word 'song' begins with a dollar sign, not an 's,'" was one of the key messages Kaiser was directed to personally deliver to the Sun Spot Records operation.

After Scott Satterfield's pep talk, which he strongly repeated by telephone, the prospect of finally getting the attention of one of Music City's top record producers thrilled Rhonda. But it also sent cold chills through the young woman from Darden, Alabama, as she finally broke down and explained to Ava Dale. "Sure I'm pleased. But I can't help but be anxious, you might even say afraid, because, Ava Dale, there are some really scary people out there. I've heard plenty about the darker side of the country music thing. What if Kaiser's got some part in that?"

Chuck Kaiser was, indeed, complex and not to be crossed. Somewhat aware of Kaiser's hard-nosed side, Satterfield thought a risk, if any was there, was worth taking. In his studied analysis of Rhonda's situation, Satterfield had determined anything would be better than remaining with Al Wendell.

In many ways a mental midget, Kaiser made up for his lack of depth by using his brass and intimidating manner to many peoples' advantage, particularly his own. He was in Nashville only a short while when he realized he needed an ally on the inside of the town's financial innermost circle, which ran the city. The opportunity presented itself when he met Ed T. Pirtle, whose victims knew the "t" stood for "take." Despite their many successes, the two men were driven to constantly seek new sources of profit, and, if they had their way, one would be named Rhonda Haynes.

When Satterfield had mentioned the stunning redhead to Kaiser, Kaiser's instructions were to go to her immediately and see if she would be interested in making a move. Kaiser made it clear that a meeting was to be arranged as soon as possible before someone else could get to her. Satterfield jumped at the chance and soon delivered Kaiser's quest.

When Rhonda arrived at Chuck Kaiser's office on Music Row, a week following her meeting with Satterfield, she was thinking about all that had happened since she'd met Al Wendell and, more specifically, about all that actually hadn't happened. She'd paid for two demonstration tapes, but nothing ever materialized except for several singing engagements at juke joints where amateur night was just "an excuse to sell longnecks to rednecks at half price," as she described it to Ava Dale.

And, there had been that urgent telephone call from Darden.

CHAPTER 10

"Rhonda, you know I don't like to call you at work, because I know you're busy, but the girl, her name's Ava Dale or something like that. Anyway, she said it was urgent." Dawn Wendell had called Rhonda at the Blue Note Lounge.

"She said someone had called from Darden trying to reach you," Dawn continued. "I'm not sure what's happened, honey, but whoever called for you said you needed to call the church where your mother works real quick. That's all they said or at least that's the most that Ava person told me. Do you have any idea what they're talking about?"

Rhonda thanked Dawn and assured her she knew the church to call.

"Well, call me back, honey, if there's anything I need to do. It sounds pretty bad from what your girlfriend said," Dawn said.

As Rhonda was reaching into her pocket for a dime for the pay phone to get an operator for the call to Darden, she promised to call Dawn back and tell her what was the problem. Rhonda quickly thanked her again and immediately placed the call. Her thoughts were racing in all directions. When she reached the church, the news was just as she had feared.

"Rosie, I think you need to get down here," Grace White, the minister's wife, said. "Your mother's pretty sick and has asked for you. We thought you knew, but Emma told us she hadn't said anything to you at all about her problem. It's her colon, I think they said."

When she reached Darden, Rhonda found out her mother had only mentioned to Mrs. White she was having a problem Emma thought was chronic diarrhea. Only when Emma had begun passing large amounts of blood had she finally gone to the doctor. Tests proved her problem to be cancer, which the doctor said had spread from her ovaries to her colon. Nevertheless, Emma had insisted on remaining in her garage apartment until the pain became even more than she could bear. She had reluctantly allowed herself to be hospitalized only after collapsing at McGee's Market.

When asked by Mrs. White, Emma had reluctantly agreed to let her call Rosie.

"Don't say it's bad," Emma instructed. "Just tell her I need to see her about some things, but not this, understand. I can tell her in my own way when she gets here."

Borrowing Dawn Wendell's new Chevrolet, knowing her Plymouth would not make the trip to Alabama, Rhonda drove as quickly as she could back to Darden, back to the world of Rosie Scoggins, where Emma did not yet know about her daughter's music endeavors. Rhonda's arrival at the Crenshaw County Memorial Hospital late on a Friday evening was as Rosie Scoggins, not as Rhonda Darlene Haynes.

"Mama, it's me, Rosie," she said softly, and gently touched the arm of the sleeping woman. Relieved there was no one else in the room, Rhonda at first just sat on the empty bed across the room looking at the figure who had become frailer than she could have ever imagined. Finally, needing to assure herself her mother was still alive, she walked over to the bed and touched her thin right arm, being careful not to disturb the I.V. tubes.

Slowly, Emma's eyes opened and her gray lips parted.

Before her mother could say anything, Rhonda asked, "Mama, why didn't you tell me how sick you were?"

"Didn't want to bother you, Rosie," Emma replied weakly, managing a slight smile. "I really didn't know myself, honestly. I just thought it was the heat or all those things they've been spraying on the garden these days," she explained. "I just didn't know. Besides, you've always written all those letters about how hard you're working and all. I don't ever want to be a problem for anyone, especially my Rosie." Emma reached over and clutched her daughter's arm, which was rubbing her mother's shoulder.

For a time, both were silent. Emma's eyes closed as she once again spoke. "Rosie, you've always been more of a fighter than I have. When someone treated you badly or tried to keep you down, you just kept on going. I gave in too much, and that wasn't right." She paused to catch her breath. "I never knew what else to do, didn't think I had any other choices about things, but you did. You knew the difference, that there was something better. You always have. I taught you all I knew how, but you taught yourself a whole lot more. And you're better for it, I know."

Moments later, with Rhonda still standing beside the bed, Emma's words seemed to escape from her in a weak, tired voice. "When you were little, you were always begging 'Mama, I want to go with you.' And you did," she said. Still squeezing her daughter's hand, she continued, "But what would I have done with you, if you hadn't? There was just you and me. No one else to keep you while I worked. But you were always afraid I was going to leave you or something. I guess all children feel that way at times."

Emma's eyes closed again, but she went on. "This time you can't go with me, Rosie. This one's just for me. But you'll be all right. You'll do just fine. You always have, and I've never doubted you would. My Rosie can tackle the world. In my own way, I tried to show you how. Don't ever stop going after whatever you want, Rosie. Don't ever give in." She clutched her daughter's hand even tighter. "At times I had to. You understand why. But don't you ever. Ever."

Emma spent most of the next two days slipping in and out of a coma. Rhonda remained at her mother's bedside at the hospital almost constantly, leaving only for brief moments to speak with a nurse or to get something from the hospital cafeteria. Then Emma died.

Rhonda patiently accepted the offers of sympathy from representatives of the First Methodist Church, where Emma had worked and lived all her adult life after leaving the orphanage. Rhonda arranged a simple graveside ceremony where Emma was buried beneath a towering cedar tree. "They're older and wiser than any of us, Rosie," Emma had often said of the trees when her Rosie was growing up. Several members of the church and a few of Rhonda's high school classmates attended the funeral service. They heard a hymn Rhonda requested. The old hymn had been a favorite of her mother's as long as Rhonda could remember. As Emma cleaned a home or the church, she hummed it constantly. The song was about a little child who had died. Its chorus was one of Rhonda's earliest memories:

> *Such a tiny little grave*
> *In a shady, lonely spot.*

A small gray marker
One forget-me-not.

On the afternoon of her mother's funeral, Emma Scoggins' only child drove to the apartment where she had lived for eighteen years. She wanted to collect some of her mother's belongings, and stopped by McGee's Market for some boxes.

After quickly climbing the wooden stairs leading to the second floor apartment over the garage, Rhonda fumbled with the key, then slowly opened the door. She was immediately struck by how clean and neat the place was. It had been some time since she had seen anyone's home as straight as Emma kept hers. She placed the empty boxes on the floor next to the worn brown sofa and sat down. Looking first from one wall to the next and then at the objects in the small bookcase beside the door to the tiny kitchen, she was amazed by what she saw. There was little in sight that reflected Emma Scoggins. Everything was a sign of Rosie. The photographs, the high school yearbooks, souvenirs from the county fairs. Later, in a box under her mother's bed she found every letter she had written her mother since leaving Darden. Inside a black, tattered Bible was an envelope containing a single dried, brown flower, probably a rose, Rhonda guessed. On the envelope was written the name "Helmut" in her mother's handwriting, but Rhonda saw no significance. She had never heard the name before and felt sure that the only person who might know what "Helmut" meant was now dead. She set the envelope aside to put in a box of things to be discarded, but then thought better of it and placed it back in the Bible.

Rhonda quickly began placing the few items she wanted into the boxes, and in less than an hour she was gone from the apartment. After placing the boxes in the car, she hurriedly walked over to the minister's house. She was relieved to find no one there.

She left a note for Grace White on the front door thanking her for everything and directed that her mother's remaining possessions be sold and the money be given to the Crenshaw County orphanage in Emma's name. Minutes later Darden's Rosie Scoggins was once again leaving her hometown. She was relieved to be going back to Nashville. Back to her new world—the world of Rhonda Haynes.

CHAPTER 11

The executive offices and studios of Sun Spot Records were located on the south end of Music Row right next to RCA and directly across the street from the Country Music Hall of Fame. That fabled street of dreams was populated by modern glass office buildings housing the headquarters for top labels and publishing houses, along with remodeled older homes inhabited by the less prosperous, but no less ambitious artists and their agents. An increasing number of lawyers and accountants had also opened offices on Music Row to be nearer the action.

Parking her Plymouth in a visitor space near the front door of the Sun Spot Building with its Aztec-like emblem of the sun over the door, Rhonda checked her hair and make-up in the mirror one last time. Scott Satterfield had assured her there was no need to be nervous about her meeting with Chuck Kaiser, although he had cautioned, "Kaiser may talk too fast, but he seems to know his business." In reality, she wasn't sure whether she feared Kaiser as much as she dreaded telling Al Wendell about a change in plans, if one occurred. She had been careful to keep her meeting secret and asked Satterfield to request the same of Kaiser.

Entering the Sun Spot reception area, Rhonda was dazzled by the many beautiful large portraits of some of the biggest names in country music. Bronwyn Kincaid. Donald Dillham. Corkie Rudd. Hank Luna. Anita Alvie. The Richmond Brothers. Comedian "Dingle" Berry. Those and others too far down the hall for her to see.

Rhonda was still too excited to actually sit down and didn't want to wrinkle her dress any more than she had driving to the studio, so she wandered around looking closer at the stars' portraits, until the husky-voiced receptionist told Rhonda, "Please follow me."

Kaiser wasn't in his office. The receptionist instructed Rhonda to sit down and wait. "I'm certain Mr. Kaiser will be right back. There's a recording session in progress upstairs. I'm sure he's probably checking on that," she said. "Would you like something to drink?"

Rhonda thanked her, but declined. Sitting in the red leather wingback chair facing the large, cluttered desk, Rhonda was awestruck by the framed gold records on the office walls and the many photographs of a grinning man with a gray crew cut surrounded by one star after the other. Most of the photographs were inscribed.

"To Chuck Kaiser—you made it all happen. Many thanks, Bronwyn."

"For Chuck. Quite a man and quite a friend. Hank Luna."

She was contemplating getting up from her chair to look around the room when she heard the door open behind her. Without turning around, Rhonda heard Chuck Kaiser's crisp, slightly nasal voice. "Sue, Carl Carson calls, put him through, but hold any others," he said to his personal secretary. He entered his office and closed the door.

Rhonda stood and turned. "Mr. Kaiser, I'm Rhonda

Haynes," she said, offering her hand, which he didn't acknowledge.

He walked to his desk without ever taking his eyes off her face. "Please, Miss Haynes, sit down. Sorry to keep you waiting, but there was an engineering problem in the studio and I had to check on it before this afternoon's full session," he explained. "Care for a cigarette?"

She, too, was taking note of her host. Later she told Ava Dale, "If I had seen Chuck Kaiser at the Blue Note Lounge or on the street for that matter, I'd have looked right past him. He's short, has beady eyes, and a squint I think just might mean his jockey shorts were grabbing him. And his crew cut is the first one I've seen anywhere since high school." But she kept those thoughts to herself at that moment.

"No, thank you. I don't smoke," she replied as she watched her host light his filtered Marlboro with a huge lighter in the shape of a guitar. Pleasantries over with, Kaiser leaned forward and folded his arms on the desk. "When I sent Scott Satterfield on a fishing expedition, I had no idea he'd bring us such a trophy," he began.

He enjoyed her smile and blush, and continued. "You know, seriously, Miss Haynes, if you can sing half as good as you look, and I'm told that you can deliver a song with no small amount of finesse, I'm going to owe Scott for a long, long time. A mighty long time." He laughed. "May I call you 'Rhonda'? Everyone around here calls me 'Chuck.' By the way, is that your real name?"

"No," she said with some hesitation. "Al Wendell came up with the Rhonda Darlene part. But Haynes is my real last name."

"Well, at least he did something right. The name fits and is certainly worthy of the bearer."

Feeling she should say something, she remarked, "I do love your office. You've got some very impressive friends. And they sure seem to think a lot of you."

"That's because they're nice people. I've worked hard for each one of them. Guided their careers, helped them make the right decisions, protected them from some of the traps out there. This business has attracted more than its share of undesirables. Nashville may be Music City to most people, but to a shamefully large group it's in danger of becoming the con capital of the entertainment world. Now don't get me wrong. There are some awfully fine people in this business. I'm not badmouthing any particular persons. I'm just saying some of us try harder and do more for our clients than some others do or even try to do. And that's what I want to talk to you about."

"All right," she replied.

For the next hour, the very confident CEO of Sun Spot Records asked questions and felt sure he knew most of the answers. "Are you married?"

"No, I'm not."

"What all have you been doing since coming to Nashville, aside from working with Wendell? What I'm asking is how have you been supporting yourself?"

"Mostly I've been waiting tables at the Blue Note. For a while I lived with a friend to help with expenses. Then I moved in with Al and Dawn, pretty much for the same reason."

"Let's get to the crucial question, Rhonda. Just how serious are you about a career? It's a lot of hard work," he warned.

"I know that. That's why I'm here today. You can definitely believe I'm willing to work."

Convinced about what she said, Kaiser asked a more

practical question. "Do you have a contract with Al Wendell?"

"Yes. There's a contract."

"Do you recall when it will expire?"

"I haven't looked at it recently. But I feel pretty sure there's about a year left."

"In my opinion it's a year you can't afford to waste," he said. "Rhonda, if you're interested in seeing what we can do for you, I'll have to buy out that contract from Wendell and quickly. Before he can get into a commitment that might ante up the price even higher than I can imagine it already will be. He's not a total fool by any means. But I'm willing to do that, if it won't present too much of a problem for you. First, though, Rhonda, I want to outline what I have in mind."

He propped up his feet on the desktop and began a litany of services and benefits. That is, if she signed with Sun Spot. He reminded her of what he had done for other entertainers. "All that and more, if my instincts serve me correctly, can be yours. That, however, will depend on you. How hard you work and how well we work together." The last part he clearly emphasized.

Before she could respond, he added, "I know this all sounds appealing, at least I hope it does." He laughed. "But there's a great deal of dedicated effort involved in what I've described. And not just a little blind faith. You've got to trust me and the people around me. But, according to what Scott told me and what I can easily see for myself, where you're concerned, the sky's the limit, as they say."

Rhonda was more than eager to make a commitment. "You know I've been living with the Wendells," she said. "I'll have to find another place to live quickly."

"No, I was not aware of that circumstance, but it's not

insurmountable. Let me explain something. Something you are always to remember." He looked right at Rhonda as he lit another cigarette. "Rhonda, in this business, and I'm sure it holds true in other businesses, it's important to look successful. You have to play the success role, even before you make it a reality. And it's not just for the public's benefit you do this. Sure, how they perceive you is important. Not just how you sing, but how you look. Everything. They make your success their success. You're leading their fantasy lives for them, and you can't let them think for one minute you're not the top dog around. The people want their heroes, their stars, to be the best. That's part of it. But it's not just for them," he explained. "It's for your own sake as well. You've got to play the role even to convince yourself. It's a matter of attitude, and you've got to cultivate it and damn well live it. Every minute of every day. Hold on to it for all it's worth. Success breeds success in this business. The right attitude is crucial. The right look must be projected in so many small, but important, ways."

Rhonda slowly nodded.

He went on. "In the country music world, trappings are a big part of the picture. You've got to look and act the part of a star. You've got to have the right clothes, a decent place to live, the right automobile—everything. Each thing makes a statement about you and your success. Each one helps you live the role, project the image." He methodically detailed the rest of what was available, even necessary, for Rhonda Haynes if she came to work for him.

"Sun Spot has an apartment we keep for when visiting executives from the parent company or other dignitaries are in town. It's in a very exclusive complex near Old Hickory Lake north of town. It's fully furnished. You can have it for a few months, until your plans are solidified. When someone else comes in town, we'll just get them a fancy suite at the Hermitage Hotel or something. They won't know the difference. And we'll know you're being taken care of.

"Of course, you're going to have to quit your job at that bar downtown. You'll be under contract here, so there's no need to wait tables anymore. You'll be working here. And I do mean working," he added. Rhonda kept listening. "Until our contract matters are finalized, you'll need some cash to carry you. As part of the contract, Sun Spot will buy out Wendell's contract. But your own immediate cash needs should be handled apart from us. Until you're officially on the payroll, that is. Our attorneys insist on that and as an attorney myself I understand what they mean."

To ease any money fears she might have in the immediate future, he offered further assistance. "Listen, I have a friend at a bank downtown. I've sent a lot of people to him, and he always worked out things to their satisfaction. Why don't you go see him, borrow some money to cover you for a while? His name's Ed Pirtle. Ed's a senior vice president at First State Bank and a damn good guy to know. I'll call him and tell him you're going to be in to see him." He wrote down the banker's name and telephone number and handed the piece of paper to Rhonda.

"When are you going to contact Al?" she asked. "I kind of would like to know, so I can have all my things out of there just in case there's a problem."

"Rhonda, yes, I'll tell you when I'm calling Wendell. But there will be no problem. Believe me, I know. That's how Wendell and his kind make their real money. He finds talent, signs them to a contract, and then sells that contract to the highest bidder, if he can find one. Hell, it would scare the pants off him to have to actually do something personally to further a career. He doesn't know how and doesn't need to.

He does have an eye for talent and often for a sucker, and he lets nature take whatever course it will. You are pure, solid talent and definitely not a sucker," he assured her. "Don't worry about him or his contract. I'm sure he'll make us pay handsomely for Rhonda Haynes. And from where I sit, it just might be the best investment we've made in a long time. I'd be disappointed if old Al didn't try to stick it to us, but I know how to handle him. I know what his needs are."

Again, she asked about the timing for the call to Wendell. "Just so I can have everything where I want it and all."

"Okay, little lady, today's Tuesday. How about you working on that between now and Thursday? Then I'll give Wendell a call on Friday, and you *will* be back here in this office the following Monday for work. I'll have some papers for you to look at then. How does that sound to you?" Reaching for his telephone, he buzzed his secretary. "Miss Haynes is leaving. Give her the key and directions to the Essex House apartment. Call ahead and see that the kitchen is stocked. She'll be moving in on Friday. Have the cleaning service in there before then. After she's left my office, get Ed Pirtle on the phone for me."

The day after her meeting with Chuck Kaiser, "my future," as she described him to Ava Dale, Rhonda called the number he had given her for the bank. Friday and the move from the Wendells would come all too quickly, she knew. She wanted to have as much settled as possible before her first day at Sun Spot the following Monday.

Right after a quick stop at the lunch counter of Harvey's department store, she walked down Church Street to First State Bank. Immediately she was ushered into a walnut-paneled office and the warm handshake of Ed Pirtle, senior vice president and trusted friend of her soon-to-be new boss.

Pirtle, as everyone called him, was a wiry little man with thick glasses and a horse laugh that could be heard throughout the bank lobby if his office door was open, something not unusual due to his desire to see everyone who entered the bank. "Please have a seat, Miss Haynes. That is right, isn't it?" he asked as he took the young woman's hand and led her to a chair right beside his desk.

"Yes, sir. Rhonda Haynes. Mr. Kaiser called you, I believe," she replied.

"He certainly did, right after you left his office, I believe he said. Chuck said you were a real looker, but, frankly, that doesn't do you justice. I can see why he's so interested. About your career, that is." He laughed and snorted. Getting no response from Rhonda, he got down to business. "Chuck said you might need a loan to tide you over until your contract takes effect. I've done the same for several others in your business, and it's always worked well for them. The bank makes a dime and the loan makes your life a little easier. So you can concentrate on your singing career. That's what's important at this juncture. Chuck Kaiser's the best there is around this town. You're a lucky lady. Mighty lucky." He continued to stare.

"Thank you, Mr. Pirtle. I'm really excited about what's happening. This means a lot to me, as you might imagine," she said.

"Have you given any thought about how much you might need at this time, Miss Haynes? It is miss, isn't it?"

"Yes, sir. I've never been married." She had long ago decided to stop ever mentioning a first husband or anything else related to her past. Her mother was gone, and in her mind so was the entire state of Alabama. "Well, since I won't have to pay rent right off, and I have a car, I think I will just need enough for food, some clothes, just the basic essentials."

"How does five thousand dollars sound?" he proposed. "And I will set it up on a ninety-day note, so you can renew it or add to it, if necessary. We'll set up the repayment part when Sun Spot starts paying you." They talked a couple of minutes longer and then agreed Rhonda would come back in about an hour to sign the paperwork.

After window shopping along Church Street and browsing the cosmetics counter at Cain-Sloan, the biggest department store she had ever seen, Rhonda returned to the bank.

That time the door to Pirtle's office was shut after she was seated. Pirtle reached across his desk and handed her the simple promissory note. It was for ninety days as discussed, but she was confused by the amount. The note was for six thousand dollars.

"I thought we said five thousand dollars," she stated. "This is for more than I will probably want to borrow."

"Well, you see, Miss Haynes, you're only getting the five thousand. The other comes to me. It's sort of a fee," he said. "Miss Haynes, you need money. But who is going to loan money to a young, single woman who just quit her job? Based on Chuck Kaiser's recommendation, I'm willing to take a risk with you. No one else would, I can assure you. You do understand the reality of what I'm telling you?"

Rhonda's gaze never left the banker's face. She realized he was right, but hated what he was doing. She hated what she heard and immediately despised Ed Pirtle. Wanting to get as far from the man as she could, she quickly signed the note and handed the piece of paper back to him as if it were something unclean. In turn, the banker produced five one thousand dollar bills in a manila folder and handed it to her. "I suggest you deposit that in the account I just opened for you," he advised. "You'll need to sign the signature cards. My secretary has all the paperwork for you."

As she stood to leave, Pirtle added something new to the day's developments. "And there's one more thing," he began. "Your new boss saw you leave Sun Spot's parking lot in an older car. I believe he said it was a Plymouth. He wants you to look successful. It's part of what he likes to call 'trappings.'" He reached into his pocket and handed her a set of new car keys. "I have set the car up in Sun Spot's name for now, at Chuck's direction. My secretary will take you to where it's parked downstairs in our garage. If you want, give my secretary the keys to your car when you've gotten your things out. I assume the title is in the glove compartment. If you want, we'll sell it for you and credit the sale proceeds against your car loan. Just sign the back of the title over to the bank."

"That's fine," she said. She started to tell him the heater didn't work, but decided to let them figure those things out for themselves.

Within little more than ten minutes, Chuck Kaiser's latest discovery drove out of the First State Bank parking garage in a fire engine red Camaro convertible. The car had a white top, white leather interior, and four of the fanciest wheel covers she had ever seen. She acknowledged to herself that Chuck Kaiser was definitely taking control of her life, for the time being at least, and she decided it suited her very well. He was right about one thing, she admitted. That new car, those fancy trappings, did wonders for her image and made her feel special for the first time in a long time. On her way to the Wendell's, she decided she would tell them, if they asked, she had borrowed the car from a friend who was out of town. She hoped that would satisfy them, at least until Friday when they got the rest of the story from Kaiser himself.

"Here's something new I thought you might like to hear," the young disc jockey told his listening audience. "At least a new arrangement of an old tune we haven't heard in a while. The release is from Sun Spot Records by a new artist over there named Rhonda Haynes. She's quite a sensation, especially if you've laid eyes on her. Where was she when I was in high school and still single? Anyway, you'll remember 'Same Old Stories, Same Old Lies' from a few years back. It was big then, but wait until you hear what this gal Rhonda Haynes has done with it. Folks, this lady can tell me stories, tell me lies any old time she wants. Let's listen."

It had been decided by Chuck Kaiser personally to have Rhonda's first release be a remake of an earlier hit by another artist. "But it will be your special treatment that will get their attention. The comparison will definitely work in your favor. I was certain of that the first time I heard you sing it on that demo tape Wendell made." Acquiring the tape had been part of the contract buy-out arrangement "for one hell of a price," he had told her at the time. When the song was cut again by Rhonda with Sun Spot's top back-up musicians, Kaiser's belief in her was more than confirmed. Whatever the tune, Rhonda put her own twist on it, gave the words a unique inflection, and generally made the song her own.

Kaiser had carefully selected the material for the new tape, with some suggestions from Rhonda, and sent it to his superiors in New York. The Avanti Records executives were "super impressed," he reported to her, and were eager to see what their man in Nashville could do with her career. An eight-by-ten color photograph of Rhonda accompanied the tape and also produced quite a reaction. Another feather in Kaiser's cap.

After fleeing the Wendell residence, Rhonda spent the

next few months getting accustomed to all the close direction Kaiser provided, along with the hard work and long hours in the studio. Her new boss had indeed delivered, as promised. She had a new contract she signed without having anyone else read it. "I read it and have no complaints," she told Kaiser. "Seems like what I would imagine is standard stuff. I like what I've seen so far, Chuck. I trust you fellows."

And there had been no amorous demands from her new mentor. "Apparently, that drill sergeant wife must be doing something right. I've never heard anything about Chuck being a womanizer," Rhonda pointed out to Ava Dale.

The Essex House apartment was a real eye-opener for her. Taking in the apartment, the convertible and the clothes Sun Spot selected for the photo session, she told Ava Dale, "I feel like a million bucks, but I don't really have a cent that's actually mine." On Rhonda's second night in the Essex House, Ava Dale brought a bottle of champagne and demanded to see everything. The two had talked well into the night, lying in front of the apartment's stone fireplace, until Ava Dale realized the time.

"I better get my butt home before Mitch sends the dogs after me," Ava Dale said. Before she left, she asked whether Rhonda had met any single men at the Essex House. "I bet they're just lined up around the pool on weekends," Ava Dale predicted.

On her own, Rhonda had met someone. "He doesn't work in the music business. He's real low key, has his head on straight." And she could have added, but didn't, that his sexual appetite was just right for her needs, nothing too demanding and always gentle. A lanky, recently divorced attorney originally from Kentucky who lived in an apartment two buildings down from Rhonda's. "He's not looking for a serious commitment. And that suits me just fine," she explained to Ava Dale.

"He's just my private after work friend, and I want to keep it like that. Private. That way my business and my fun won't get all tangled. It's better that way from what I've seen downtown already. And I can handle each whenever I want to for now."

Her relationship with the attorney consisted of nights with no one else around, when both could get home at a decent hour without being too exhausted. He always came to her place because he said he got a kick out of all the fancy gadgets Sun Spot had installed. The sex was always a mutual thing, but never what the evening was all about.

The rest of the time she sincerely enjoyed her new role as a rising star and just had fun. Rhonda was quite a flirt at times, she kept them all wishing and at arm's length. She went out of her way to convince Kaiser she was serious about the business, strictly business, to let him know his investment was safe.

In the spring following her initial success on the music charts, Kaiser announced it was time for Rhonda to venture out. "I want to book you on a tour, just a couple of public appearances on a limited basis, nothing too elaborate for right now," he explained. "Just to test the waters and see what you're comfortable with before a full-fledged road trip. It'll be opening for someone like the Richmond Brothers the first time, but there'll be more later down the proverbial road." He made the announcement during a meeting with Rhonda and two junior studio executives and staff members. He was very pleased with the latest reports of success for "Same Old Stories, Same Old Lies." He beamed when he told her, "That little jewel is number one for the third straight week. Pretty damn good for the first time out." They were all congratulating each other on the success of the record and, of course, Kaiser's excellent stewardship.

"I have a few ideas in mind," Kaiser continued. "I want to keep you close to Nashville this time. Avoid the big cities in Texas, Ohio, and the like. By the way, the disc jockey association in Ohio voted you the next big star last week at their meeting in Columbus. That's not too shabby. Ohio has always been a good barometer for what works."

Turning to the chief engineer, he asked, "Are we going to have Rhonda's new single ready on time? I want it out before the album and right before this tour thing."

"No problem, Chuck," the engineer replied confidently. "What about the photo for the album jacket? I've heard some discussion about that."

Rhonda was eager to tell Kaiser about the photography session herself. "I had one photo shoot last week, but no one's exactly thrilled," she explained. "There's a guy coming in from New York the day after tomorrow with some fresh ideas. We'll see what happens then. We just didn't get the right look that first time."

"All right, people," Kaiser said. "That's enough for right now. Go back to your cages and let me talk with Rhonda a minute longer. Besides, there's too much heavy breathing in here. Might tarnish those gold records."

After the others left his office, Rhonda adjusted the hair comb she was wearing and calmly awaited whatever Kaiser had to say.

"I'm dead serious about the timing on all this," he began. "It's damned important. Your name and your talent are out there at the moment. Now it's time to put a live face with the name and the voice. The whole package, the real thing. And, God, are they going to go nuts," he said and slapped his hands together. "Absolutely crazy. You just watch." He quickly lit a cigarette and went on. "There's an event coming up in early May. I think it'll be perfect. It's right here in town, and the crowd will be so consumed with themselves at that thing that you'll be able to do whatever you please. It'll give you an opportunity on a small scale to see what works for you and the band and what may not, if anything."

Kaiser set the stage for the event. "Beginning back in the early forties, every year in the spring several thousand people get together on the side of a hill overlooking a race track outside Nashville. It's called the Iroquois Steeple Chase. Riders and horses are brought in from all over the United States for the races. But the real show is the night before at Broad Meadows County Club. The local socialites throw a big fancy party to preview the next day's races and to get a head start on the betting and their hangovers. It's black tie and customarily the evening's entertainment is some band. But I've arranged for you to put in an appearance this year."

After Rhonda's release of "Same Old Stories, Same Old lies," Kaiser was confident of its success and contacted Ed Pirtle's wife, who served as the club's entertainment committee chair that particular year. "Francine Pirtle loved the idea, said she thought a cute country singer will give the night a 'darling touch.' But she made me promise you'd be dressed properly and all. I assured Francine I know the difference between the Iroquois party and some honky-tonk on Gallatin Road."

Kaiser gave Rhonda a brief description of the physical layout for the performance and some more explicit instructions for the evening. "Just give them three, maybe four songs. Make sure 'Same Old Stories, Same Old Lies' is one of them. Might be a good idea to start with it. I'll leave that up to you. But nothing more, unless you just want to. See how it goes. I'll send out the top musicians from the studio to back you. The bands they usually have at those Broad Meadows functions wouldn't do you justice," he said. "And be nice to Ed Pirtle," he reminded her. "He's powerful in this town, and he's been a friend of mine for a long time. He and his wife will definitely be there that night. When you meet her, be sure to thank her for arranging this."

Rhonda momentarily entertained the thought of telling Kaiser about the loan and what kind of a friend Pirtle really was, but decided not to bring it up. In all honesty, she thought, she really didn't want to know if her boss actually knew how his banker buddy operated.

"All the local swells and their ladies will be there," he went on. "Speaking truthfully, the bottom line is they don't give a rat's ass about country music. Few would ever admit they could even name a country song. Their idea of slumming is to get all tanked up at someone's dinner party and then drag all their friends downtown to one the beer parlors on lower Broadway to giggle at the tourists and listen to 'that music' as they call it. But don't get me wrong, Rhonda. They're actually nice people. Just unrealistic about how important this industry is around here. It pays more than a few of their salaries one way or another, whether they want to admit it sober or not. And this business does occasionally need their financial wherewithal." He paused and then cautioned, "They're nice, but not harmless. Definitely not harmless."

CHAPTER 12

The night of the party at Broad Meadows Country Club on the eve of the Iroquois Steeple Chase, Rhonda arrived at the club alone. She had told Kaiser she did not want to be driven. "Hell, it's just across town, and we'll be out of there early. I'll meet the musicians there around nine o'clock," she said. When she drove her red Camaro up to the front door of the country club, a man in a starched white jacket, black trousers, and white gloves promptly opened her car door. Handing him the car keys, she reached behind her for the make-up case on the backseat. "I'll be back before too long, so you won't need to park this too far," she said, trying to be helpful and not wanting to have to stand in line and wait for her car to be brought back to her when she left. "I shouldn't be here more than an hour and a half or so."

Another club employee, similarly attired, graciously opened the door to the foyer. Instantly, she was approached by a sober-faced man in his late thirties. "You must be with the band," he observed, not smiling. "I'm the assistant manager, Michael King. Please come this way. The orchestra still has a few moments before they take a break."

Rhonda immediately saw what Chuck Kaiser had told her. Some people, the assistant manager for one, were eager to see a difference between the orchestra and her band.

"Your people are waiting in the manager's office. This way," he gestured as he turned. Rhonda followed him across the crowded foyer and down a hallway.

Rhonda heard the deafening roar from the ballroom and realized even the orchestra was probably having trouble being heard. Entering the small office as directed, she welcomed the prospect of getting away from the noise, at least for as long as she could. The drummer, guitar player, and the studio's new bass player were waiting, as promised. She could see they, too, were relieved to see a familiar face.

"If you should need anything, I'm Mr. King and—"

"Yes, Mr. King, that will be just dandy," Rhonda interrupted. "What would you fellows like? I'm going to have a bourbon and water."

No one in the tiny office was particularly surprised when Mr. King didn't return immediately with their drink requests or at any time soon after for that matter.

When Mr. King did return, much to their dismay with no drinks in hand, he announced it was time for them to set up. Later, Ava Dale got an earful about what Rhonda saw when she and the band entered the ballroom of the country club and hurriedly set up their instruments. "Ava Dale, trust me. I couldn't wait to turn around to see what was making all that commotion. What I saw was a room full of a bunch of broadly grinning men in tuxedos and loud, braying women in more yards of crepe and net in more colors than I could have ever imagined, except maybe at a Crenshaw County High School prom. It looked like the fabric department of that Parks-Belk back in Montgomery had thrown up. They were all seated around fancy round tables, white tablecloths and plates of food scattered everywhere. You wouldn't believe the mess."

Without asking Rhonda or her musicians whether they were ready or not, the assistant manager walked to the microphone, adjusted it to Francine Pirtle's level, and left the stage. Still holding her dinner napkin, Mrs. Pirtle walked to the microphone and began her prepared remarks. "Ladies and gentlemen, I trust each of you is having a perfectly delightful time this evening. My committee and I put in a lot of work—" She was interrupted by brief applause. "Thank you. The entertainment subcommittee chaired by Mrs. Horace Doolittle is proud to present local recording star Rhonda Darlene Haynes from Sun Spot Records right here in Nashville."

Those introductory remarks were followed by pockets of scattered applause. But the chatter from the party crowd didn't noticeably subside. There were, however, whistles directed at the terrific redhead.

Throughout her performance, there were polite instances of applause at the appropriate times. So she knew someone had to be listening. She did four numbers, finishing with "Same Old Stories, Same Old Lies," as Kaiser emphatically insisted on. After the fourth song, Rhonda waved to the crowd, then instantly left the stage and the ballroom.

Waiting in the hallway, drink in hand and obviously not his first of the evening, was Ed Pirtle, mule grin, thick glasses, and all. Rhonda remembered Chuck Kaiser's words. "Be nice to Ed Pirtle. He's powerful in this town."

Rhonda walked up and spoke first. "Why, Mr. Pirtle, I didn't know you'd be here tonight. Thought you'd be downtown guarding all the bank's money."

"No, no. We have a whole army of guards for that job," he responded. Laughing, he tipped his glass and spilled some of its contents, but never noticed. "I go out of my way not to miss a good party, especially this one. It's always great year after year. Must be spring and everybody's anxious to get out again. But this one's even better with you here."

Rhonda smiled politely.

Stepping closer to her, Pirtle dropped his voice, although no one else was in the hallway at that moment. "Let me ask you something, sugar. The guys at my table were wondering, does that red hair go all the way down? You know the old Chinese saying, 'Woman bleach hair on head still have black hair by cracky.'"

Rhonda pondered his comment for only a moment. "Let me tell you something, you skinny little creep. I took your thieving crap that day at your office in your high and mighty bank, but I'm not taking any more of it. Now if you think for one second you bought anything that day, you're sadly mistaken. I'm not collateral for any damn loan you ever made or ever will make. And if you so much as lay one of your slimy hands on me, I'll go back to that damned microphone, and it sure as hell won't be a love song I'll be singing to your fancy friends. No, sir. It'll be a real uptempo number and up your skinny ass." But she wasn't finished. "Now let me tell you something else, Mr. Pirtle. I've put up with quite a few jerks in my life. Some have even been cute enough to get by with it. A couple I might even say were worth the trouble. But you, sir, are not cute and definitely not worth the trouble. So why don't you take your pathetic balls back into your party and try to find someone willing to put up with you and your crap. I'm a lady so I can't tell you what I'm really thinking. But it rhymes with *fuck you*."

Confident she had gotten her message across, she quickly snatched the drink from his hand and poured it down the front of this tuxedo. "Good night, Mr. Banker. And thank you so very much for everything." She walked down the hallway, first stopping to retrieve her make-up bag from the manager's office, and made her way to the front door.

Driving home, Rhonda was still shaking and angry. Talking to herself, she said, "If anyone thinks they own this one, they're dead wrong. They're going to need me much more than I'll ever need one of them. Any of them." She was almost shouting. "Rhonda Haynes is nobody's property. And if the bastards can't figure that out for themselves, I'll just damn well tell them in words of one syllable."

CHAPTER 13

Eighteen months had passed. Rhonda and her band were on the road in the third week of one-night performances taking her from Scottsdale to Raleigh with fourteen stops in between. Personally designed by Chuck Kaiser, the tour was to promote her album entitled, *Just a Heartbreak Away,* her second in as many to go platinum. That was accomplished in a record-setting eight days.

Rhonda had worked hard for the recognition being heaped upon her, coast to coast. In the minds of many industry insiders she was soon to be the top female in country music. But her achievements were at no small price. In her opinion, she had become a commodity to Sun Spot and, in particular, its CEO, marketed in a way benefiting the label mostly.

The long hours demanded by Kaiser had brought her more success than she had ever envisioned in her wildest dream and, in some ways, less happiness than she desired. Her lanky attorney "friend" had left her for what she suspected was someone more frequently available. She was constantly in the studio, on a talk show, or on the road. There was just no time she could find for a personal life, but she was willing to make the sacrifice so long as she felt appreciated. "Ava

Dale, appreciation is so damn basic. And it's so wrong if it's not there in any relationship, business or personal. Without that you're just a convenience, a simple whore."

The hotel key said "The Greenville Holiday Inn." Greenville, South Carolina, the last tour stop before Raleigh two nights later. The telephone in Rhonda's room rang, and it was Kaiser calling from Nashville, so she took the call. Only in major cities like Atlanta did she perform twice in one evening to accommodate the demand for tickets. That meant the evening after the show in Greenville would be a free one, and none too soon for her and the band. She was close to exhaustion and needed to protect her throat. Kaiser's call couldn't have come at a worse time—or perhaps his timing was perfect. At the minimum in her mind, it could force the inevitable, depending on what he had to say that was so important.

Kaiser went straight to the point. "I want to add another night's performance in Raleigh," meaning she and the band would have to forfeit the scheduled night off. They needed to leave immediately for Raleigh.

"Look, Chuck," Rhonda began, after listening silently to his message. "You've got ten tired, and I do mean tired, musicians and sound crew here. This has been one damn tough schedule from the start and the bad weather didn't help one bit. And then there's me. At the risk of sounding ungrateful," she continued, "I think what you just proposed stinks. In fact, it stinks real bad. Sure, I know ticket sales are important. I'm not saying they're not. But at this point of this particular tour, I'm not so sure it makes a whole hell of a lot of difference. What's a few more dollars going to say in the long run?" He tried to interrupt, but she wouldn't let him. All the months of holding back spilled out. "Or maybe that's not something you've considered or even thought about at all. I say this tour ends as planned or it ends right here."

Her ultimatum was followed by silence on the other end of the telephone line. Then Kaiser carefully selected his words. "Rhonda, I realize it's been a tough three weeks. But in my judgment this one change is not going to be the end of the world for anybody."

"No," she snapped. "It's going to mean the end of a lot more than you might think. I've truly had it, Chuck. You've been pushing for a long time, and this time you've gone too far, as I see it. You really have. I definitely didn't need this call, along with a lot of the other crap that's been shoved my way lately. Like that last song I couldn't stand. But, oh no, it had to go on the album so you could pay back a friend. Hell, tonight you didn't even have the courtesy to ask how I was. It's all just money to you."

"Look, Rhonda. You're just a little off base here. No, make that way off base. I shouldn't have to remind you what you owe me and this record label. You were waiting tables and running from an ex-con named Al Wendell not too awfully long ago, if I remember correctly. Or just maybe your memory isn't long enough."

"Oh, it's long enough all right. Long enough to know my opinion has never mattered on anything. I've been treated like a piece of choice steak you let the world nibble on, and I had about as much to say about it as the stupid cow it came from. And, one more thing. Your high and mighty friend Pirtle's a crook—a simple, slimy thief."

"Goddammit, you either do another gig as I said or your fucking contract is going to have a new clause in it when you get back. Don't forget, bitch, I damn well own you."

"What?"

"You heard me. I said you're acting like a goddamned ungrateful bitch. Want me to repeat it again?"

Those were the last words Chuck Kaiser ever said to Rhonda Haynes.

She hung up. Then she immediately dialed the room of Carl Sutton, her tour bus driver. She knew Carl was also fed up with the grueling tour schedule and a number of other things at Sun Spot Records. "Carl, can you come to my room?" she asked. "Yes, I know what time it is, but this is damned important. We need to talk. Kaiser just called me, and the shit's really hit the fan. Please?" She knew "please" always got to Carl Sutton. He heard it so seldom at work.

After relating the entire conversation with Kaiser to Carl, they made a pact and decided to risk everything. Their plans were to have Carl call Raleigh and cancel her appearance for what they would call "health reasons." Being a big fan of Rhonda Haynes, the Raleigh agent promised to take care of everything there the next morning.

Then Carl called his older brother who lived just outside of Greenville and borrowed a truck. They realized they couldn't take the tour bus and strand the rest of the group, so a borrowed pick-up truck was the answer. "I'll get it back to you," Carl promised his brother.

As agreed, Rhonda and Carl took a cab to meet his brother at the Waffle House on Highway 37 outside Greenville. Only the person driving the truck wasn't his brother. Behind the wheel was a good-looking young man who appeared to be in his mid-twenties.

"Who are you?" Rhonda asked, looking first at the stranger and then at Carl for an answer.

"I'm a friend of Carl's brother. He got tied up and said you were going to Nashville. I thought I'd just tag along, if you don't mind being crowded."

Rhonda thought he was damn good-looking.

"I've always wanted to get to Nashville, show some of my lyrics to real pros. As long as the truck's going that way, I thought I would, too. I like to write songs and all and figured Nashville is the place to be. This one bag won't take up much room. And I'm willing to help with the driving, if you want."

"What's your name?" Carl finally asked.

"Curtis Harmon. But my friends call me Dusty."

The three of them drove straight through, stopping only for gas and "people fuel," as Carl called it. When they drove up to her apartment at the Essex House, Rhonda got out of the truck and walked quickly to the front door. She was back immediately.

"The bastards must have changed the locks," she announced. Glancing over to where she had left the studio's Eldorado convertible, she saw it too had fallen prey to the wrath of Chuck Kaiser. The car was nowhere to be seen. "Damn. Those jerks do play hardball. Carl, take me to a pay phone," Rhonda said. At the Gulf station two blocks away, she called the one person she was confident might have an idea about what to do next. She was relieved when Scott Satterfield answered on the first ring.

"Scott, it's Rhonda. Yes, I know what time it is, but I need some advice. Kaiser and I have parted ways. Big time. It's been brewing for months, probably ever since I signed his contract, but I think that thing's a thing of the past." Satterfield asked what happened, and she told him. "He's been pushing me, pushing all of us and when he demanded—didn't ask, *demanded*—we stay another night in Raleigh, I just let him have it. He got an earful about everything that's been bothering me. So we had words and now I'm back here and they've changed the locks on my apartment and my damn car's missing."

Satterfield only said, "Whoa."

"Okay, genius. What do I do now?" Rhonda inquired.

Satterfield knew he needed time. "Rhonda, I need to sort through this. Give me twenty-four hours. Call me back here tomorrow night after eight o'clock. My advice now is to go a hotel. Register under another name in case Kaiser starts trying to find you. He won't want to let up the pressure. He's good at that, I'm sure. Call me back and let me know where you are. I'll wait here till then."

She thanked him, agreed to do as he said, and hung up. Mindful of the time of morning, but knowing he had to act, Satterfield immediately called Avery Springer. Springer was head of Athena Records and was known for his savvy in handling artists and all the related complications that inhabit the music business. More important in Satterfield's mind was Springer's well-earned reputation for being fair and universally respected, a rarity in their business. Satterfield definitely didn't want to jeopardize his own relationship with Rhonda Haynes. He was convinced her career would only soar higher and had longevity, another rarity in the music world. He was equally confident Avery Springer was the right person to work with the now-famous redhead. On a couple of occasions, when he was around the Sun Spot studio, he had sensed some tension between Rhonda and her boss, but had said nothing about it. Her call came as no surprise.

Carl echoed Satterfield's advice when he heard it from Rhonda. "I agree. You better go to a hotel until things settle down a bit." After a few minutes' discussion, they decided Carl would take Rhonda to the Andrew Jackson Hotel downtown. "I'll sign in using my name. Kaiser won't be looking for me just yet," he said. "I don't think you're in any real danger as such. But Kaiser must be super pissed and can be pretty mean when he's crossed. I've seen it before. I need to get over to my place and check back with the band. I told Ronnie before we left I'd call back and tell them to get back here. Ronnie's driven the bus before."

Thinking about Dusty Harmon for the first time since reaching Nashville, Carl suggested Rhonda let Dusty stay with her while Carl took care of other matters. "Might be a good idea for Dusty to stay in the hotel, too. I'll get him a room near you until we get you more settled. I'll use Sun Spot's money to pay for both rooms. That ought to really piss Kaiser off even more." For the first time all night, Rhonda and Carl both laughed.

Rhonda agreed and so did their new friend, who was "just along for the ride anyway," he reminded them. Carl drove directly to the Andrew Jackson, which was two blocks from the Hermitage and less frequented by music industry people. He got the keys to adjoining rooms and gave one to each of them. When he saw they were on the elevator, Carl left and drove home.

Entering the suite, Rhonda headed straight to one bathroom with her cosmetics kit, while Dusty opened the door joining the two rooms and disappeared into the other room. Half an hour later she emerged from the bathroom rubbing her hair with one towel and wearing another. Even though it was almost mid-morning, she heard "Good night" from the other room. After closing the curtains, she turned down the bed cover and fell into it.

Adjusting her pillows, she turned out the light, trying not to focus on the events of the past several hours, but couldn't avoid them. She closed her eyes, struck by the fact that she was in another strange bed and in the next room was a young, handsome man.

Only he wasn't in the next room. He was sitting on the

side of her bed gently rubbing her bare shoulders. The light from the bathroom was still on and she saw he was smiling that same smile she had seen when he first jumped into the pick-up in Greenville and signed himself on for the trip.

"Am I bothering you?" he asked in a South Carolina drawl.

"No, that's fine. It's been one hell of a trip. Feels damn good in fact," was her response.

She turned to face him and told herself the prospects were promising. Seeing her expression and appreciating the thoughts behind it, without another word, Dusty Harmon eased into the warm arms of Rhonda Haynes and into her life.

Following their marriage several weeks later before a justice of the peace, Dusty quickly turned out a series of song lyrics like none Rhonda had ever heard. Almost immediately their combined skills made them a formidable duo on Music Row. Rhonda enjoyed two giant back-to-back hits using her husband's magic words. "Just Touch Me" set industry records for time at the top of the charts.

But Dusty had a different kind of habit that caused her anything but joy. Night after night the harsh truth about Dusty's other interests became the dominant part of their reality. At first she denied what she saw, not wanting to admit there might be a problem. She concentrated on her work, but even that wasn't possible when Dusty missed important recording sessions and some nights didn't even come home. Eventually, she realized she couldn't hide the situation from anyone, particularly herself. Dusty had a fondness for cocaine, one he could not control, and it affected everything he did. Eventually, Rhonda made a stark acknowledgment— her second marriage was becoming as rotten as her first.

CHAPTER 14

"That's got to be it for now, Avery. I can't look at another sheet of music right now. We've all been at it for God knows how long today. What do you say we come back tomorrow morning early and listen to what we've done so far? If anything needs fixing, we can do it then," Rhonda said. "That cut we did right after lunch will definitely need some tweaking. I can do better than what I felt was coming through on that one."

Everyone in the recording studio agreed that it was time to take a long break from what had been a marathon session. Rhonda and her closest associates had been at the Athena Records studio since early that morning working on her new album. "I'm determined to release it before summer," she stated, so the session's length came as no surprise to anyone. The song she said she wanted to work on was one of Dusty's. She thought it had the potential to be huge. The song was about "making love songs, instead of making love."

Everyone had made it to the recording session the next day. Everyone except Dusty. Rhonda left their new home that morning before Dusty. She had told Avery she wanted to be at the studio earlier than anyone else. "I want to try a few things by myself with a couple of songs without having anyone around." Aware of her wishes, the studio head had a driver pick her up at seven that morning.

Before leaving her home she left a note by Dusty's car keys where she knew he could find it. The note simply said, "Be at the studio as soon as you can. I need you." But he never showed up and her calls to the house between breaks went unanswered. She eventually stopped trying to reach him around noon.

Avery consciously made every effort to shield Rhonda from stress, especially when she was in the studio. He had insisted Carl Sutton drive her to town that morning, and it was Carl who drove her home later that afternoon right after the draining recording session.

Carl guided the Athena limousine to the front door of Rhonda's home, the one she and Dusty had just purchased and moved into. It was in a secluded part of Wilson County, just a few minutes' drive east from Nashville. Both Rhonda and Dusty preferred to avoid the usual route taken by music industry people, who built flashy, oversized houses in Hendersonville or Gallatin. The couple had chosen a large turn-of-the-century farmhouse they then remodeled. The location allowed Rhonda to keep two, maybe three, Tennessee walking horses, her newfound passion. The only horses she had ever seen growing up in Darden had been workhorses or an occasional mule. She was dazzled by the elegance and grace of the horses and spent as much time as she could with her prized possessions.

"Don't get out, Carl," she instructed. "I'm tired, but not completely helpless. I'll see you right here in the morning about the same time as today, if that's all right with you."

Rhonda got out of the limousine. She stood there for a minute as Carl drove out of the long driveway. Then she looked over and saw Dusty's Corvette, a gift from her when she first took one of his songs to the top of the charts. The song had gone gold in two weeks' time, so that was the color she chose for the sports car. But she noticed the car was parked much too close to the boxwoods by the front door. And the driver's door was not completely closed, leaving the interior lights on.

Slowly, she walked to the car and shut the door. "Now who does he think will jump start this thing if the battery runs down?" she muttered to herself as she turned to go inside the house.

There were no sounds when she opened the door and stood for a moment in the foyer. Normally, when Dusty was home, there would be at least the stereo and one of the televisions blaring. This time she was greeted by total silence. She placed her large tapestry handbag on the table in the foyer and went to the kitchen. After pouring a cold glass of tea from the refrigerator, she walked to the den. There was Dusty sound asleep on the overstuffed sofa; his boots were on the floor nearby. He was breathing heavily. Beside her sleeping husband was an open bottle of Wild Turkey and a partially filled brandy snifter on the large antique trunk they used for a coffee table. On top of a recent issue of *Billboard* magazine was a short straw and a single-edged razor blade. Rhonda did not look any further.

Preferring to let him sleep it off and just get away from him at that moment, Rhonda went upstairs. After working all day, she mostly wanted a long, hot shower and a few minutes of quiet. Certain the next day would be equally demanding, she wanted to be in top form. Anything less she would find unacceptable. As she came out of the bathroom, she was combing her still wet hair when she saw Dusty leaning against the bedroom doorway with both hands in his jeans pockets. She hadn't put on a robe.

He offered no excuses for failing to show up at the recording session. And without asking her how the day had gone, Dusty smiled his smile and walked to the bed. Moving across the room, he removed his shirt and took off his jeans. Rhonda was not amused and still resented how she knew he had spent the day, but the prospect of a roll in the hay with Dusty still had its appeal. She couldn't deny she needed a physical workout to offset her mental fatigue. Placing the comb on the dresser, she walked to the bed and joined him under the comforter.

She wanted to take advantage of Dusty's obvious high before it was lost, so she took control. Once it was clear he could perform and she had not been cheated by the mixture of cocaine and alcohol, she moved on top and directed his every move exactly where she wanted.

Suddenly, he snapped and shoved her aside. Standing beside the bed and staggering at first, he shouted, "You just have to be on top, don't you! Hell, Rhonda, you're always on top. You're on top of the whole fucking world. You're in control of our damn relationship. Always have been. What in the hell makes you so damned set on controlling everything around you? What in the hell did that to you?"

Momentarily, she was stunned. Then without responding and aware he wouldn't remember a word she might say, she got up from the bed, grabbed a robe, and went back to the bathroom. When she emerged from the bathroom, she was relieved to see Dusty was asleep and headed to the guest room for the night.

The next morning Dusty surprised his wife. He was up and downstairs before she was. He had prepared coffee and toast with her favorite strawberry jam. When she entered the kitchen, he didn't look up, only said, "I've made some break-fast, if you want it."

She didn't acknowledge the plate of food or the coffee on the countertop. "I've asked Carl to pick me up. He'll be here any minute. Maybe it would be better if you stayed here again today," she told him.

"I thought you said you needed me for the session. That's what you said when it was planned." He was looking at her, but realized she wanted to have as little as possible to do with him.

She slammed her handbag down on the countertop, sending the plate of toast flying onto the floor. "Oh yes, indeed. I said I needed you. I most definitely did. But it was yesterday I needed you. And it was the old you I wanted to be there, not the stoned, no-show bastard you've turned into."

Ignoring what she said, he asked, "Don't you want something to eat?"

Rhonda could control her anger no longer. She slapped his hand away from the coffee cup. "No, dammit. I want you!" she shouted.

"Well, we can go back upstairs."

"What do you think I'm talking about?!" she screamed, shaking her head in disbelief. "That I want to . . . hell, I can't even say it anymore. No, you fool, what I want, or at least wanted," she was trembling, "is the same man I married, the man who could make me crazy with love just at the sight of him, the man who knows me and who I am as well as I do, and who, I thought, even loved me for who I am. I wanted to share my life with someone who made music matter, made it more than just work." She tried not to cry, but lost the battle. "But what you seem to overlook is that it doesn't matter whether you're selling vacuum cleaners or used cars, making biscuits or firecrackers, it's business. It's always a business, and you don't let anything get in the way. Nothing. Not booze. Not drugs." Bluntly, she added, "Not even love."

For the first time, she saw tears in his eyes and waited for him to say something. In all they had done together, crying wasn't one of those things until that moment. "Look, Rhonda, I know I've been screwing up. And I know it's hurt you, hurt what you do. But, goddammit, you're not the only one that can get hurt. Last night when you were on top of me, I . . ."

"You what?" she shouted. "What in the hell happened? What did I do? Tell me."

"It wasn't you. Something you did reminded me of a bunch of crap."

"Well, what the hell crap do you mean?"

Thumping his chest, he went on, "I know I've hurt you, but this one's been hurt, and long before I met you. Until then, there wasn't a whole lot of good things in my life. Matter of fact, my life was pure shit. I know I've never told you a whole lot about me, how I grew up. Heard a lot about you, but kept me to myself. You know why? You want to know something? If I had stayed in Greenville, I probably would have ended up in a fucking prison."

Dusty was sobbing. "You see," he paused to wipe away tears. "You see, my stepfather sexually abused me when I was a kid. And what you did just brought it all back all of a sudden. Sure, when my mama found out, she divorced the son of a bitch. Then, you know what? She ran off with the next man who came along, leaving me with my grandmother to raise. When Carl Sutton's brother took me on and gave me a job to keep me in school, I was on the street and planning to kill my stepfather if I could find him. Lucky for him and probably lucky for me the bastard had left town by then. Burt Sutton took me in, gave me a home, and kept me from

God knows what." He stopped and wiped his eyes on his sleeve. "Then I met you." He looked at her for the first time.

Rhonda stood there, trying to comprehend all that she heard. "Why hadn't you told me about any of that before?"

"And all those love songs I write, all those times you— yes, you—inspired them, they just eat at my gut. I don't think I really know what love is. Probably never have."

She couldn't say a word. Her throat was throbbing. Stepping over the broken plate and toast, she put her arms around his neck. Holding her sobbing husband, she finally spoke. "I'll call Avery and tell him we're on the way as soon as Carl gets here. Just running a little late."

For more than a week, things went smoothly. Dusty was at the studio every day. He managed to deliver another set of lyrics, so-so in Rhonda's opinion, but at least he was working. The lyrics could be fixed, she knew, but she still had fears about the marriage. Then one night Dusty didn't come home. About two in the morning he called from a pay phone. He was slurring his words and making little sense. Rhonda answered, but had little to say during the call. When she later unloaded to Ava Dale, she acknowledged, "Why say anything at a time like that? He wouldn't have heard a word I said. If he was one of those rockets we keep hearing so much about, he was so high he'd burn out when he reached the damned atmosphere."

Two days later, when she found a small bag of cocaine behind the stereo, Rhonda wasted no time. She called Avery and asked the name of a divorce attorney. "Avery, when it's over, it's over. I don't need to talk about it, even think about it any longer. I've made my mind up. In fact, you might say Dusty did it for me. It's a business decision and nothing more at this point." Or so she convinced herself at the time.

CHAPTER 15

"Honored guests, citizens of Darden, and guests from all over this part of our lovely state, today we're here to pay tribute to someone who has gone on from here to become one of the world's foremost entertainers." Hearing those booming words, Rhonda was convinced the ordeal she had dreaded but felt she had to endure, was actually happening, even though she had vowed it never would. She had just been introduced to her hometown crowd by the beaming mayor of Darden, Alabama.

Rhonda was standing before one of the largest crowds she had seen in a while, and was equally certain it was the largest crowd in the history of Darden, except, as she later told Ava Dale, perhaps the time when the Crenshaw County Wildcats played the Montgomery Central Bulldogs for the state football championship her senior year. As she stood and waved to the applauding throng assembled on the Darden public square, she thought back to when Avery Springer first told her about the invitation.

"Avery, old buddy, there's just no way on God's green earth I'm going back there for anything. I don't care if those fools have declared July 18 as Rhonda Haynes Day. No, sir, no way. Maybe a hundred years after hell freezes over, and then I might still have to think about it. You're actually telling me Whacker Rawlins is the mayor down there?" she said and doubled over with laughter. She then related to Springer the story of why "old Whacker had to hold a book over his crotch" in the yearbook picture.

Springer loved the story, but still encouraged her to make the trip to Darden.

"Rhonda, now please listen. None of us ever really enjoys going back. Home may not be so bad. What's so bad is being reminded of a lot of demons or just plain crap we've spent years trying to forget, even overcome," he said, sounding sympathetic.

"Oh, don't get me wrong," she responded. "I've never forgotten. And I have no intention of ever forgetting. You've seen that poster with the old Confederate rebel waving a gun and flag and saying 'Forget hell.' Well, give him red hair and you've got me and my sentiments exactly when it comes to Darden, Alabama," she said. She was pacing angrily around his office.

"I understand. Believe me, I do. Growing up in Corpus Christi, Texas, wasn't any trip to the Disneyland," he said. "But think about it this way. All those people who you obviously would rather not see are still living their drab little lives in Darden. Probably the most daring thing they've ever done in that town was install traffic signals. Or elect the high school jerk-off king mayor." With that she had to laugh.

"Mayor Whacker," she said, slowly savoring each word. Thinking she might be warming to the idea, Springer continued his efforts to put the idea in a better perspective for her. "They've all stayed in Darden, while you've gone on to become a major force in the entertainment world. Now it's your chance to go back, just for a few hours, and just plain gloat."

"All right, genius, since you put it that way. I can understand what you're saying. But I'll only do it my way."

"Always," he assured her.

"Okay, Avery. Go ahead and call his highness, the mayor, and tell him how delighted I am to attend, but I won't perform. Period. I'll be on the reviewing stand or whatever they call those things, if they even have one, and say a few words. That's all. Or I may just stand up and give them all the finger. Just kidding. I'll behave," she promised.

Rhonda also insisted on making the five-hour drive by limousine. "The longest, shiniest one you can find in this town," she instructed Carl Sutton. "I intend to make a grand entrance. Something like the one Elizabeth Taylor made when she entered Rome in *Cleopatra.*"

Arriving in Darden as close to the designated time as possible, she asked Carl to drive her past the First Methodist Church before going to the courthouse on the town square. "See that garage back there behind the church, Carl? Well, there's an apartment on the top level, up those wooden stairs on the side. That's where I grew up. Just my mama and me. Boy, wouldn't she be flabbergasted by all this now. Especially this thing today. She wouldn't believe it for one minute. But knowing me as she did, she just might after all. She was one fine lady, Carl. A real survivor. She taught me a lot, a whole lot."

When the limousine finally pulled up behind the reviewing stand the city had erected on the shady side of the courthouse lawn, Rhonda opened the door herself, only to find a balding man with a pot belly standing there holding his hat and grinning a familiar grin.

"Rosie, we're just so pleased you could come. Everyone's pleased as punch you're here," he said.

Stepping out of the limousine, after a moment she recognized Ronnie Rawlins. Smiling, she said, "It's good to see you, Whacker."

Startled by the nickname, the mayor of Darden lowered his voice and informed her, "No one calls me Whacker anymore, Rosie."

"And no one calls me Rosie," she responded.

The parade ran for more than an hour ending with the Crenshaw County High School band and flag bearers. Standing before the dignitaries on the reviewing stand, the band played "Stars Fell on Alabama." The mayor whispered to the guest of honor, "I chose that song myself. You being a star and all." The band members then took their seats in the folding chairs in front of the wooden platform draped in red, white, and blue bunting.

Mayor Rawlins then introduced his former classmate to the hometown crowd.

"Honored guests, citizens of Darden, and guests from all over this part of our lovely state, today we're here to pay tribute to someone who has gone on from here to become one of the world's top entertainers. I'm sure she's carried with her all these years the memories of her childhood here in our fair city. Just as each of us who knew her has carried in our own hearts a loving picture of her. We have in our own way shared in her success, but we're truly honored and thrilled today to welcome her back to Darden where it all began for her. Ladies and gentlemen, my good friends all, it is without a doubt my sincere, great honor to introduce someone we are all awfully proud of, our own Rhonda Haynes." Turning to face the guest of honor, the mayor led the long and enthusiastic applause.

Rhonda finally stood up, acknowledged the cheers with a wave, turned and smiled at the mayor who had returned to his seat. She stood beside the podium waving grandly to what she thought had to be half the population of southern Alabama. "Thank you. Thank you," she began, having moved back behind the podium and still waving. "Thank you all so much." When the applause and whistles ended, she began her prepared remarks. "Thank you, ladies and gentlemen. And thank you, Whacker, for that wonderful introduction," she said, then turned to the mayor and winked. Rhonda noticed a small commotion from the direction of the mayor's aged mother, who was seated on the platform in a wheelchair.

"And that band. My goodness, you all have to come up to Nashville where we can really put you to work." Again, the crowd responded with approval. "I have never seen so many people in Darden before. I'm sure the Chamber of Commerce is very pleased, but no more than I am," she lied. "Darden, Alabama, is such a special place, and I am grateful for this day and certainly for this great honor."

All the way from Nashville to Darden that day, Rhonda had ranted and raved as they drove into rural Alabama. She had kept Carl entertained with stories about growing up in Darden and they were not exactly the sentiments she was expressing to the crowd before her on the courthouse lawn.

When she finished her remarks, the high school band played the theme from *Rocky* as Rhonda graciously walked across the stage one more time, stopping once or twice to shake the hand of someone she thought she recognized. She waved and blew kisses with both hands as she descended the wooden steps. She then walked directly back to the limousine without ever looking back.

Quickly, she entered the car and told Carl, "Let's get the hell out of here."

On the way out of town, she had Carl stop by the cemetery where she placed red roses she had brought from Nashville for her mother's grave. Getting back into the limousine, the tears slowly began as she once again headed out of Darden.

CHAPTER 16

Sonny Boyd Everett's enthusiastic drawl was still holding forth on FM 108 as Carl turned the stretch Cadillac into the driveway at Honeysuckle Haven. Sitting in one corner of the backseat, Rhonda again turned on the radio hoping to hear a weather forecast for the big night ahead.

"It's two-thirty on country one-o-eight, and we're spending the entire day with three of the country music chart's finest surefire residents—Rhonda Haynes, Okalene Harris, and the new kid on the block, India Robbins. Since early this morning, and I sure hope you've been with us the entire time, we've been playing these ladies' hits—the songs, the music, the magic each one has given us to earn that nomination for Entertainer of the Year at tonight's Best in County Music Awards.

"You've just heard 'The Finer Things,' one of India Robbins' latest chart toppers. Now I want to take you back a ways. All the way back to 1968. That was the year Rhonda Haynes first won the Top Female Singer Award, and, before I play the song that had a whole lot to do with getting her that prize, I'm going to let you hear the fabulous redhead accept that award. It was the night of April 10, 1968 at the

Ryman Auditorium and here's what a breathless Rhonda Haynes had to say."

"Oh, my. This thing's heavy. And so beautiful, so very beautiful," she said and paused. "I know I'm supposed to thank a lot of people right now, and I know I should. They've done so much for me. They've always been there when I needed them, and, God knows, I've needed them plenty of times. But this one," she said, holding the trophy over her head, "this wonderful honor tonight, this award," again she paused, "I want to share with my mama. She's not here, but, Mama, I know you'd be proud of your little girl. Just like I was always so proud of you." She paused again, started to go on, but stopped, looked up, and holding back her tears finally said, "Thank you. Thank you so very much. Everybody."

"Here it is, folks," the announcer jumped right in, "the big one that earned Rhonda Haynes the Top Female Singer Award, her very first time. Here's 'Hollyhock Daydreams.' Now just sit back and treat yourself to this one."

As the song ended, Carl stopped the car at the front steps of the mansion and the rain had stopped. Now fully recovered from the ordeal with Dusty at Athena's studio, Rhonda turned off the radio. As she left the car, she leaned back in and told Carl, "We'll probably leave for the awards show early, about five-thirty or so. I want to stop by Avery's party on the way, before we go the Opry House. One of us will call you and let you know pretty soon what time exactly, Carl, as soon as we hopefully can decide on the time and, that, of course, depends on how long it takes me to get all this together. So I better get my buns on upstairs right now. Can't wait to see you in a tux again," she added and laughed, knowing how much her old friend hated to wear anything but jeans and a flannel shirt.

On her way through the foyer, she heard the stereo playing in the study and thought Roger had to be in there. Sure enough, as she stuck her head in the doorway, Roger's booming voice called out, "Okay, step around here, lovely lady. Let me see all of you. Need to make sure you're still in one piece."

Rhonda took a giant step into the room, teasingly assumed a General Patton pose with both hands on her hips, and said, "Check it out, buster." They both chuckled.

"How'd it go?" he asked, relieved to see his wife was in a good mood. Any encounter with her cocky ex-husband inevitably presented a problem, at least in Roger's way of thinking, based on past experiences.

"It went fine, honey. Dusty had a couple of songs. One of them sounded pretty promising. He calls it 'Loving in Your Lying Arms' or something like that. Anyway, I told Scott to get with Dusty and some of the musicians and work it up. We'll just have to see what happens with it," she explained. "Ruth here yet?"

"Yes, she is," he replied. "She's upstairs already. She got here with three of the biggest boxes I've ever seen and a bunch of hang-up bags she was treating like eggshells. I offered to help her cart it all upstairs, but she insisted no one was touching anything until you got back. You better go on up and start going through the goodies. What time do you plan on leaving here tonight?" he asked. "I intend to put off getting into those new tuxedo shoes as long as I can."

"I told Carl it would be about five-thirty, but we'll have to see how long it takes me. Whatever you think, though. If we're going by Avery's party before the show, we should leave early, just in case there's a traffic problem. There's all that construction on the interstate, and you know how much that can screw up traffic, particularly if it's raining, and it still looks like it might. Have you talked with Avery about the party? I didn't want to bring it up at the studio with Dusty around. Avery usually keeps Dusty at arm's length, and that definitely wouldn't include having him at the party."

"No, but I'll call him in a few minutes. He's probably still at the studio, or I'll catch him at home."

"Did you see those flowers?" she asked, pointing to a huge arrangement of fresh cut flowers in a gleaming crystal vase and wondering who had sent them. They were sitting on the baby grand piano in one corner of the room.

"I looked at the card," he confessed. "They're from Al Wendell."

Al Wendell, she thought, as she blew her husband a kiss and left the study without going over to the flowers. They were beautiful, she had to admit, but she told herself that was due to the florist, not Al Wendell. All of her memories of Wendell were anything but beautiful. To herself she remarked out loud as she climbed the staircase, "They're really coming out of the woodwork today. First, Dusty, now Al." *Next would probably be the mayor of dear of old Darden bearing a key to the city he could just shove up his silly ass.*

"Ruth, where are you?" Rhonda was halfway up the stairs when she loudly called out to her dear friend and advisor. Reaching the top and turning down the hallway toward her bedroom suite, she called out once more, "Ruth, I need you and fast."

She had gotten rid of the funk Dusty had put her in earlier in the day. She was anticipating the awards show that evening and every little detail, all she had to take care of to be ready. Convinced it was the most important awards show of her career, she insisted everything had to be perfect. For that, she depended on Ruth Staggs. Rhonda had never forgotten Chuck Kaiser's advice, "Rhonda, it's crucial to always give the impression of success," and she knew that included the right clothes. More affectionately, she recalled her mother's words. "Rosie, you may not know all the answers, but you can look good." Rhonda made it a practice to do both.

A mass of blonde curls peered around the doorway of Rhonda's bedroom when the mistress of Honeysuckle Haven turned the corner. Laughing, the petite blonde yelled back at her friend, "If you scream like that one more time, I'm going to put itching powder in your bra."

"And who says I'm going to wear a bra, Miss Smarty," Rhonda cracked. Both laughed, knowing Rhonda always wore one. "I prefer to leave the swinging tits routine to Okalene Harris," she remarked, as she frequently referred to her rival whenever cleavage came up in a conversation.

Both Rhonda and Ruth were relieved to see one another. Rhonda immediately sank into the tufted pink chaise lounge near the door, while her friend walked over to the portable clothes rack where three enormous hanging bags were prominently displayed.

Ruth immediately began her show-and-tell presentation. "I brought three outfits for you to choose from. From past experiences, I wouldn't dare risk just one. Tonight you can just bet there will be everything from black lace to brushed denim at the Opry House. Anything from terrific to ultra tacky. You know, those wild combinations of everything imaginable and couples who look like they dressed for different parties altogether."

"All right, genius," Rhonda began, kicking off her shoes. "Let's see what's on tonight's menu. Which reminds me—I'll have some sandwiches sent up here while we get this organized. I'm starved." Rhonda got up from the lounge and spoke into the intercom to the kitchen. "Peggy, can you bring us two tuna fish sandwiches with lettuce and tomato on light toast? And extra pickles. Some Fritos. A Dr. Pepper for Ruth," she said looking to her companion who nodded approval. "And a Mello Yello for me."

Walking back to the chaise, she said, "I started drinking those things when I first moved to Nashville and I just can't stop. So help me, I've tried." Before sitting down she immediately went back to the intercom and asked the cook to "remind Roger to eat something before we leave. The evening will be a long one, and he can be such a bear when he doesn't eat. Just take him some kind of sandwich, and he'll be fine. Nothing too spicy, Peggy." Turning to Ruth, she added, "I sure as hell don't need for Roger to have gas tonight of all nights."

Ruth was already standing by the clothes rack, anxious to start her own show. From the first clothes bag she carefully lifted a strapless white dress made entirely from heavy Belgian lace and lined with light green silk. The dress had a tight skirt split on one side to the top of the thigh, allowing the green silk lining to flash dramatically.

Returning the white dress to the rack on a hanger, the proud designer next brought out an emerald green satin blouse with long, billowing sleeves and an open, round neckline cut almost off the shoulder. The blouse was matched by skin-tight satin pants in the same eye-catching color, always a favorite of the star. Rhonda felt emerald green made her red hair "even redder." The pants would be so tight, she thought she might be glad she hadn't eaten since breakfast and had second thoughts about the tuna fish sandwich, or at least the Fritos, when lunch arrived. With the pants, Ruth matched a two-inch red leather belt with a heavy gold buckle.

Ruth's final creation was a flaming red gown in silk, which reminded Rhonda of "something Peggy Fleming would be afraid might melt the ice." Again, billowing sleeves, but this time with a collar cut up to her neck and the back cut halfway down to her hips. The somewhat full skirt was cut short to the knees in the front and ankle length in the back with a red ruffle all the way around the hemline.

Still reclining with her feet propped up on the chaise lounge, Rhonda was absorbed with each creation as Ruth held them up, first showing the front and then the back. Rhonda was pleased, as always, with what Ruth had produced. "You sure don't make it easy for a girl," was her initial reaction. "They're all wonderful, just fantastic. All my best colors. And my emeralds will look great on each of them." On their honeymoon Roger had given his bride a stunning emerald and diamond necklace with dangling earrings to match.

After several moments contemplating the clothes before her, Rhonda remarked, "Shoot, Ruth. I can remember when one dress like that was more than I thought I could ever have for my own. When I started in the business, I couldn't afford a damn bandana to match a blouse. Ruth, get that long white feather boa thing. It's hanging in there somewhere," she indicated, pointing to the closet. She recognized each outfit was nothing short of fabulous. In Rhonda's opinion Ruth never failed to come through. Aware that the Best in Country Music Awards show was never the happy hunting ground for the world's ten best dressed, Rhonda concentrated on making a statement that evening, determined to be seen as "the only real class act in the place."

Ruth returned from the closet with the boa and walked over to the dress rack, waiting for Rhonda to say more. "I was thinking the green pants and blouse might use something else," Rhonda observed. "Something dramatic. What do you think?" she asked.

"I think you're right. It'll work real well. And it'll give

you something to do with your hands. You always get so nervous at one of these things. You can fool with it while you
fidget," her friend pointed out. No matter how kind the crit-
ics were or how confident her closest advisors were, Rhonda
always remained apprehensive. She always agonized that
something she wanted might be taken away from her.

"Okay," Rhonda said, rising from the lounge and stepping over the ottoman. She kicked her shoes out of the way
as she reached to unbutton her blouse. "Let's see what these
look like on me. I want to try the red one first."

Several changes and trips to the wardrobe closets later,
she made up her mind. "Don't you think this does it?" she
proudly indicated. She was standing before the full-length
mirror. Her reflection showed the emerald green blouse and
pants, the gigantic white boa, the emerald jewelry, and the
green spiked heels Ruth had had dyed to match.

"That's the ticket," Ruth agreed.

"Now for my hair," Rhonda emphasized.

"Rhonda, darling," Ruth said, "the look I have in mind
is a head on a matchstick. An emerald green matchstick.
Only lit and blazing."

"That ought to get a few flash bulbs going," Rhonda
laughed. "Do you think there's anything we could do for
poor Roger?" she teased. "He doesn't have a whole of lot of
hair left and he hates these things enough as it is. Now he's
having to go with an emerald torch. Maybe he should carry
a fire extinguisher in his tux pocket."

Amused at the image, Ruth said, "He's always proud of
you, whether you're ablaze or not. And, yes, he probably
would tote along a fire extinguisher if you asked."

At that very moment, Roger stuck his head in the bedroom door. "Look, ladies, the man himself is heading to the

showers. Any last minute instructions before I turn into Cary Grant?"

"Fat chance, old buddy," Rhonda teased. She came out of the dressing room wearing a robe and quickly walked to her husband. Placing both arms around his neck, she needed to know, "Did you tell Carl what time he should be ready for us?"

"Yes, your highness. And he will be here right on the money," he said confidently. "And don't you start getting in a nervous twit. Then I'll get nervous, and we'll both be miserable if that happens."

"And no more martinis before we leave, mister," she said, smiling. The gin on Roger's breath was more than a hint. "I promise you can fortify yourself at Avery's."

"Yes, ma'am." With that he slapped her butt, causing her to squeal with delight and run back across the room where Ruth was observing the whole scene as she had so many times in the past. Quickly, Rhonda blew Roger a kiss with both hands as he disappeared down the hall.

It was a few minutes after five o'clock when Rhonda came down the winding staircase at Honeysuckle Haven. Roger was waiting in the study as she appeared at the door and just stood there. He looked up from his newspaper and did a double take. When she knew she had his attention, she slowly turned completely around. There was no expression on her face. The Queen of Country Music had never looked greater and she knew it. So did her adoring husband. Ruth was standing behind Rhonda and gently pushed her into the study.

An emphatic "shit" was his first remark. The ultimate compliment from the only man who she felt had loved her as much, if not more, than she thought possible. "Come on over here," he motioned with his hand as he slowly let the newspaper fall to the floor. The "blazing torch" crossed the room like the royalty she knew she was, stopping in front of his chair. "Do you think we could hit the hot tub real quick before we go?" he asked and ducked as she swung one end of the feather boa at him.

"No," she laughed, "but it'll be here when we get back," hoping that prospect alone could keep him awake the rest of the evening. "Where's Carl?"

"He's waiting right outside. Let's get this thing going."

First, telling Ruth good night and for the thousandth time how much she appreciated all she had done, Rhonda then took her husband's hand as the couple walked through the foyer and out the front door where the car was waiting.

The traffic was slower than normal for a Monday night, just as Rhonda had predicted, so the drive from Hooten Holler to Nashville took longer than expected, but neither of them voiced any objection. They weren't especially anxious to get to Avery Springer's home where they knew a lot of people would be waiting to wish her well. In actuality, she was confident the party would only add to her anxiety and Roger's discomfort with the whole evening. That was Rhonda's world, and he rarely entered it willingly, preferring cattle shows to awards events.

Halfway to Nashville, she leaned forward and turned on the radio. Sonny Boyd Everett was continuing his awards show marathon and still "playing the greatest of the great ones."

A well-placed music industry insider, the disc jockey had just finished a biographical sketch of India Robbins, the youngest of the three nominees for Entertainer of the Year.

"Roger," Rhonda asked as India Robbins' biggest hit, "A

Guest in Your Heart" began, "have you ever met that one?" she asked, referring to Robbins.

"No, but I did see her on a talk show the other night," he replied.

"What did you think? I mean really, what was your opinion?"

"Well, I liked her song well enough," he answered pensively. "But she seemed kind of distant or something. You know. She never smiled much or anything. She was just there. You know what I mean?"

"That's exactly what I'm talking about. Hell, that's the coldest bitch I've ever met in my life. I'll bet there's icicles hanging from that twat. The girl's cold as a fish. That's all there is to it."

"And sings like a nightingale," he observed.

"Yes, dammit. She can sing. I'll give her that one. She's got terrific range. But I still think she's dead from the neck down. Maybe it's all that long hair of hers. Maybe it just drains all the feeling out of her," she speculated and laughed, dragging out the word "drains" for emphasis.

"Yes siree Bob, ladies and gents," the voice on the radio broke in at the end of the India Robbins hit. "It would take quite a bit to top talent like hers. Some have said India Robbins has the purest sound in the business. But her competition tonight is formidable, which you already know, especially if you've been listening to FM one-o-eight all day.

"Now Okie Harris, last year's winner, is up for the big one again this year. And, of course, the legend herself, Rhonda Haynes, whose string of hits seems endless, is back again in the running. Rhonda's up for the top honor tonight, as well, and here's one of the main reasons why. It's her latest and has been at or near the top of the charts for six weeks now. It's a cut off her last album you all know went platinum.

Let's listen to 'The Other Woman' by the one and only Miss Rhonda Darlene Haynes."

"Remind me to tell him to stop using that silly middle name. No one ever does it anymore, and I probably never should have," she told her husband. The car was silent, except for the music.

> *Night after night I've poured the wine*
> *Only to stare at yours and slowly sip mine.*
> *I've been far too understanding far too long*
> *Always waiting for your call.*
> *Now read the writing on my wall.*
> *Look in my crying eyes and try to understand*
> *I can't be the other woman*
> *When for me there's no other man.*

CHAPTER 17

Four students from a local college were stationed just inside the gate of the serpentine brick wall surrounding Avery Springer's estate in Williamson County, ten miles south of Nashville. Each young man had careful instructions about valet parking the guests' expensive cars and were told to call the house if someone not on the guest list showed. Chauffeur driven limousines were given special directions to a separate area of the grounds.

"Go ahead, Miss Haynes," one beaming valet driver said, "and good luck tonight." Rhonda had lowered her window to say "hi" to the young man she recognized from other such occasions at the Springer's. Frequently, the head of Athena Records preferred to escape the distractions of the office and Music Row itself, so he hosted special gatherings at his home where he had installed a small, but complete, recording room adjacent to the elaborate pool house. These "meetings" were particularly popular during the summer months when everyone usually ended up spending as much time in the pool as in the recording room. Joan Springer's special buffets were also a welcome addition on those occasions when the Springer's opened their home to friends and business associates.

The party before the Best in Country Music Awards was eagerly anticipated by everyone who knew the event would be even more special and well worth the short drive from Nashville, Hendersonville, or Brentwood, where many industry big names lived. Avery billed the party as the "appetizer before the main course out at the Opry House."

The floodlights mounted in the trees around the home gave the scene a warm, inviting glow. Carl let Rhonda and Roger exit the car at the front door before he turned the keys over to one of the parking attendants.

"Carl, you come with us. Avery insists," Rhonda said. The couple considered Carl as "family." Avery was well aware of that and always acknowledged the sentiment.

When the door opened, the Springer house was bursting with life. Laughter, screams of southern delight, and the aroma of bourbon filled the air. The host was preceded by two large black Labrador retrievers who bounded from the house in search of squirrels who frequently raided Joan Springer's collection of bird feeders hanging in the lighted trees. "Lord, Rhonda," Avery exclaimed, "you're not playing fair tonight. All the other ladies will have to go home and start all over again. Damn, you look nothing short of fabulous." Gently hugging his number one star, he proudly ushered the honored couple into the huge, richly appointed living room, where a large crowd of guests anticipated the arrival of the one and only Rhonda.

Before relinquishing Avery's welcome arm, Rhonda whispered, "Have someone bring me a light bourbon and water and get poor Roger a gin martini up before he collapses." Avery laughed and turned his prize guest over to his wife. Within seconds the noise level was again up to a roar. All praise and well wishes for Rhonda. Over the marble mantle they had hung a banner reading—"RHONDA, WE

Love You!" A tape of instrumental arrangements of all her top songs played on the stereo system throughout the house. Her smiling face was featured prominently in the many awards in the bookcases and in the photographs atop the grand piano.

Several minutes later, Roger was "ready to get on with this thing. Don't you think we ought to go on out to the Opry House?" he asked.

"Not just yet," she replied, somewhat pleased to see he was still nervous, an indication he had limited his martini consumption. "Some people are just now arriving. This is an important night for Avery, too," she reminded him with a soft pat on his cheek. "We'll have plenty of time," she assured him as she waved to Bill Pete Tucker and his new wife who had just entered the room. It was, indeed, a very big night in the country music world. No one intended to miss a single moment of the action.

Eventually, Rhonda again found the host and hostess at one end of the living room talking with a record producer from the West Coast. "Don't you think we all ought to make our way to the awards, Avery?" she suggested after accepting a good luck kiss from the grinning producer. She carefully made sure his greasy hair came nowhere near hers.

"I think you're probably right," was his answer. "Why don't I have both our cars brought around so we can leave first? Everyone else can stay as long as they want and follow later. But we do need to get there. The press will want to talk with you before we go in, I'm sure." Within ten minutes Carl was driving Rhonda and Roger back into Nashville and across town toward the Opry House. The Springers followed with Avery piloting his new silver Jaguar convertible, a birthday gift from his wife.

The Opryland theme park was situated alongside the Cumberland River, which wound its way through downtown Nashville and on to points west. Five miles east of the city, the park itself was a conglomeration of the usual theme park rides, various music halls for country music performances, souvenir shops, a small petting zoo, and eateries for all sorts of food from Tex-Mex to "down home, southern fried," as the signs boasted.

The soul of the park was housed in the Opry House itself. Built in 1974, the new home of the Grand Ole Opry replaced the aging, but still sacred, Ryman Auditorium downtown. Housing a state of the art television and sound production center, the vast new auditorium served as Mecca reborn for country music greats, near greats, hopefuls, and their legions of adoring fans. Every Saturday night throughout the year, each seat in the Opry House was filled, along with a set of wooden bleachers kept backstage for local dignitaries and visiting VIPs. Each show was unique, a tribute to what millions of the faithful believed to be America's best contribution to the world of music.

It was Tuesday night, not a Saturday, and the crowds were again pressing to get a glimpse of all their favorite stars gathering at the Opry House for the colorful extravaganza known as the Best in Country Music Awards. The fans standing outside and the lucky few inside had voted weeks earlier, along with others across the nation, for the musicians, singers, and writers the fans considered simply the best. That acknowledgment of their respect and excellence was cherished by industry people who would personally greet the public the following day at an elaborate autograph party at the Country Music Hall of Fame.

"If I can get through this tonight, everything else in my

life will be a piece of cake, or at least might seem like it," Rhonda remarked as Carl guided her Cadillac through the main entrance to the facility's grounds. "I'm an absolute nervous wreck."

Reaching over and taking her hand she had braced against the seat, Roger said, "Well, if you think this is something, wait until I get you back home in that hot tub."

Smiling, she replied, "I don't know if it would be better for you if I win or lose. Either way I'm going to take it out on your tired, old body." She laughed, appreciating his attempt to help her relax.

"I'll take my chances," he responded just as Carl stopped the car at the front entrance to the Opry House. Floodlights were scanning the sky and the flash bulbs resembled fireflies in a swarm. Carl had earlier arranged for someone else to take the car so he could go in with Rhonda as she had wanted. "Carl, you have sat outside too many times. This time you're going in and sitting with us," she had insisted. "You've been getting off way too easy," she teased, knowing he had been through it all with her for years. She wanted to show her appreciation of him where everyone could see, all thirty million of them.

Not waiting for anyone to open the door, grandly emerging from the car, Rhonda was greeted by camera flashes, television lights, and sharp applause from people she couldn't see, being blinded by the flashing lights. She stood beside the open car door and waved as she waited for her husband and Carl to come around. Taking Roger's left arm and an embarrassed Carl's right hand, the three of them moved toward the doors to the auditorium and encountered a second round of lights and screams.

Rhonda stopped before the first microphone thrust toward her. She smiled broadly, waved again at the cheering, whistling fans, and waited to be asked how she felt about the evening. "I'm Greg Stone, WTGY News, and I'm here with the very glamorous Rhonda Haynes. Miss Haynes, how do you feel about the evening? You're up for Entertainer of the Year, as if you had to be told. What does that feel like?"

"As if you needed to remind me," she responded. "Oh, I feel great. Being here and being nominated is honor enough. We'll just have to see what happens in there. The fans are so wonderful," she said and waved again, "and I love them all." The three then linked arms again and playfully started toward the door once more. Two additional stops were required before they finally reached the building lobby. An Opry House page assigned to show them to their seats waited just inside the door.

Avery and his wife were already in their seats next to Rhonda's three, which were reserved on the second row from the front, center stage. The Springers had used a rear entrance to the building to avoid the hullabaloo at the front, but Rhonda had insisted on making an entrance. "The fans want to see me, and I damn well need to see them, too, if the truth be known," she admitted.

Avery stood and motioned for Rhonda to sit on the aisle. "No," she politely declined. "I want to be on the inside. Carl, you take the aisle seat, then me, then Roger next to Joan. I can just climb out in a hurry if I need to," she directed. "And I damn well better have to," she added. That sentiment did not have to be said. It was well understood by everyone around her.

Within a short time, the lights briefly dimmed signaling the awards show was about to begin on time at the network's insistence. The orchestra launched into a medley of songs chosen as "Song of the Year" for every year since the late 1960s when country music had leaped out of the trailer parks and pick-up trucks and gained a respect of its own on a much wider national scale.

Ten minutes later the master of ceremonies, Art Pickens, proceeded to the guitar-shaped Plexiglas podium to begin the night's presentations. Terror immediately struck Rhonda when she saw the long flight of stairs "some sadist always dreams up" for everyone coming on stage to descend. "Somebody ought to send those bastards who design sets for award shows to a special hell. They're just dying to see someone fall down those stairs in front of millions of people," she whispered to Roger, but loud enough for those around her to hear. "And look at those stairs we have to climb to get on stage from here. A stupid mountain goat would need lessons."

"Now calm down, babe," Roger said, patting her hand. "You'll do just fine. Just fine."

As the polite applause for the master of ceremonies ended, the evening finally began. "As your host this evening, it is my distinct pleasure to welcome all of you who are here and the many millions of fans all across the globe to the twenty-second annual Best in Country Music Awards presentation. These are the awards lovingly bestowed on your favorites by you, the fans. In many ways, it's really your night. And quite a night it is going to be." Another burst of applause was followed by the first award of the evening.

"To present the award for Best Male Vocalist is a gal who herself is a nominee for Entertainer of the Year tonight. Ladies and gentlemen, Miss Okalene Harris."

Without a pause or even a downward glance, Okalene Harris quickly walked down the middle of the long, curved staircase, confident she would not have a problem making the descent.

"Look at her," Rhonda practically gasped. "She looks like

a nun." And others around her had to admit the similarity. The most famous chest in country music was nowhere in sight. Okalene Harris was the picture of forced modesty as she walked across the Opry House stage in a full-length black dress with a high collar, white French cuffs, and a hint of a white ruffle around the top of the collar. "Roger, she's never looked like that in her life. She knows something. Someone's tipped off the bitch. She knows. I know she does," Rhonda said in a panic. Her worst fears seemed about to come true. Okalene Harris was going to get the award and a whole new world of respect along with it. "She's either found Jesus or a better seamstress, or both, since I last saw her," Rhonda remarked.

In soft, measured tones the picture of innocence standing at the microphone grandly announced the nominees. "The nominees for Best Male Vocalist are Hank Carlson, Jerry Hardin, and Cliff Van Zant." Each name was welcomed by bursts of scattered applause.

Rhonda was still suspicions. "Hell," she whispered to Avery as she leaned across Roger and Joan, "she's even talking differently. What's happened to her Oklahoma twang?"

Opening the envelope, Rhonda's chief competitor breathlessly provided the name of the winner, "And the award goes to Cliff Van Zant."

Rhonda smiled approvingly and applauded along with the rest of the audience, but her mind was still doing cartwheels. Okalene Harris' sudden transformation into Julie Andrews with the Boston Pops had taken Rhonda by surprise and heightened her anxiety.

Five awards later, the first of the three songs nominated for Best Song was performed by India Robbins. The song, "Breaking in a New Broken Heart," had been recorded by

India, but the nomination was more a tribute to its legendary writer, Chet Hunter. India's appearance didn't have the same effect on Rhonda as Okie Harris' had. When India Robbins came on stage, Rhonda gathered her feather boa around her and remarked to Roger, "I swear the temperature in here just dropped twenty degrees. God, she's an iceberg." But her suspicions about Okalene Harris hadn't subsided. Rhonda was convinced her old rival had been tipped off and would walk off with the Entertainer of the Year Award for certain.

At last, her opportunity to work off her nervous energy arrived. When she got the cue, Rhonda left her seat to present the award for Best Female Vocalist. As a two-time winner of the award in previous years, she was pleased when asked to make the presentation. The awards show was well into its second hour, and Rhonda's tension level hadn't diminished since the first award and the startling appearance of Okalene Harris.

"Thank you. Thank you very much," Rhonda said into the microphone as the thunderous applause, easily in her mind the loudest of the evening to that point, continued. She was actually relieved to finally be at the podium and thrilled to hear the warm, sustained adulation from throughout the cavernous room. Having successfully made it down "that damn staircase" slowly but regally, the famous redhead appeared relaxed. When her signature brush of her right hand through her hair only started the applause and whistles all over again, she knew she hadn't lost her legendary ability to control an audience. Scott Satterfield had called it "presence" and presence it was.

"The nominees for Best Female Vocalist are Anita Alvie, Adrienne Whitley, and Randie Carson." Beaming as the audience responded to each name, she took the envelope, opened it with a flourish, and loudly announced the name of

the winner. "Ladies and gentlemen, it's Adrienne Whitley."
When the winner rushed on stage, she was embraced warmly by Rhonda and her flowing boa. In Rhonda's opinion
there was no comparison, and she hoped everyone else took
note. While Adrienne Whitley was a gifted singer, Rhonda
admitted to herself, her denim shirt and matching vest
trimmed in leather were not in the same league as Rhonda's
emerald elegance. Rhonda was relieved to acknowledge at
that single moment she was feeling better already. The
encouragement from her fans affirmed who she really was.
Then a cold thought struck her. *The votes are already in and
that damn Okalene Harris knows something,* she thought. By the
time she returned to her seat between Roger and Carl, her
nerves were back in full force.

After Lewis Alexander accepted his award for Best Song
for "The Reason Is," there was only one award left to be presented. The host announced, "To make the final presentation
the Country Music World Association's board of governors
has asked Brick Webster, the popular mayor of Nashville, to
give out the award for Entertainer of the Year."

Rather than attempt an on-stage entrance by way of the
treacherous staircase, following his introduction, the mayor
entered stage left, absent his trademark cigar, but proudly
giving the world a chance to see the equally famous swagger
of someone a local newspaper writer had once observed
"took walking lessons from John Wayne. And he even wears
cowboy boots." Webster's black boots, polished to a patent-
leather sheen, were guaranteed to make him look taller than
his five feet eight inches. Proudly standing there in his tuxedo and plastered black hair, the two-term mayor of Music
City grasped the podium with both hands and began his presentation with a few remarks about the importance of country music to the world and particularly to Nashville. "I would

be remiss," he said, "if I didn't stand before you and sincerely acknowledge the immense contribution of country music
and the industry to the reputation and, most certainly, the
economy of this city."

Finally, he proceeded to the award itself. "The three
nominees for Entertainer of the Year have each already been
up here tonight. They are Rhonda Haynes, Okalene Harris,
and India Robbins." Again, each name was followed by
applause. There was then a buzz throughout the auditorium,
followed by almost total silence, as the mayor removed the
white card from the envelope. He paused as he read the card
and then looked up smiling. "Our Entertainer of the Year is
Miss Rhonda Haynes."

Brick Webster's words, as later described by Roger, were
followed by something resembling a cross between a frenzied
rodeo crowd and the prolonged welcome of a popular president to the floor of the House of Representatives for the
State of the Union message. Rhonda later had to admit, "It
was wild and it was wonderful."

She sat there stunned for only a brief moment. First, after
quickly kissing her husband and then Avery Springer and
finally Carl Sutton, she stepped into the aisle. She walked easily up the steps and was received by the grinning mayor.
Then she turned and faced the audience, only to ignite once
more the firestorm of adulation. For the first time in many
days, Rhonda Haynes relaxed. Gazing at the crystal and
bronze award with deep affection, her first words confirmed
what a few, if not many around her, already understood. "If
only you knew what this means to me." She hesitated, then
continued. "I honestly can't tell you or anyone here on this
earth how much this business can take out of you, if you're
serious about it, and God knows I am." The audience
laughed and briefly applauded. "But it's worth it when you,

our fans, give back so much in such a wonderful, touching way." Setting the award back down on the podium, she resumed speaking with soft assurance. "My mama once told me that giant cedar trees are older and wiser than any of us. I know what she meant, and she was so right. Growing up, I once carved my initials in a big old cedar tree. And years later I went back and saw that the tree had done its darnedest to erase the evidence of my intrusion. Unlike many youthful memories which once were gold, but later turned to sand, I've seen a lot of things that have taught me a good many lessons, just like that cedar tree. But the greatest lesson is revealed by how you live, how you treat other people. I've always been grateful for the many kindnesses shown me in this business. And I've always welcomed each and every opportunity to return those favors. Tonight is one of the greatest ever, and I owe all of you. Thank you. Thank you. All of you. I love you." With those words, she left the stage, once again on top of her world and determined to stay there for quite some time.

Backstage the first person she saw was Scott Satterfield. Bypassing all others, including the eager press, she walked up to him and immediately asked, "What was that one song you and Dusty are going to work on? The one we heard this morning."

"'Your Lying Arms,'" Satterfield answered, amazed she was even able to think about anything at that moment.

"That's it," she said. Nodding at the award she clutched in one arm, she explained what was on her mind. "Well, this means we have even less time. You know I have to follow this with a real chart buster, and, Scott, it can't be six months from now. I want to get to work on it as soon as possible."

"Trust me, I do understand," he replied. "Dusty and I will

get together tomorrow, the next day at the latest. I understand what you want, and you'll have it. I promise."

She kissed him on the cheek. "I know you do. You always have, and I love you for that. And tell Dusty to get his ass in gear, too." With that she turned and gave a brief interview to her favorite disc jockey. The one and only Sonny Boyd Everett had continued his marathon at the awards site. She was soon joined backstage by Roger, Carl, and the Springers.

Her husband walked up behind her and whispered. "You aren't taking that thing into the hot tub with us tonight, are you? Looks deadly. Someone might get hurt."

"If you do get hurt, I guarantee you'll enjoy every minute of it," she teased, drawing him nearer with her free arm as the feather boa slipped off her shoulder. "Let's see how fast Carl can make that Cadillac run. I definitely need a workout."

CHAPTER 18

Rhonda wrapped her robe loosely around her as she left her dressing room at Honeysuckle Haven. The emerald outfit and feather boa were draped across the chaise lounge, and the award had been placed carefully on her dressing table. She was on her way to the hot tub where she was confident she would find her husband. In her private thoughts the evening had been truly rewarding in so many ways, a triumph for her by any estimation. But at that moment she needed to be less of a star and more of a woman, something Roger would understand all too well.

When she first met him, by many standards Roger Keithe was a tremendously successful gentleman farmer. He fiercely maintained that a person should be more valued for what they earn personally than by what their "daddy leaves them or a rich wife might provide." A quality he shared with Rhonda. With a great flare for prize cattle and beautiful, accomplished women, his first wife had died of cancer several years before he knew Rhonda, met the music star, courted her, and married her, all within less than a year.

Rhonda had originally been amused by the tall heavy-set man in the white Stetson who had asked a friend in her business to introduce them. Her fame and success didn't intimidate him. He only saw a truly beautiful woman and sensed he saw beneath her famous facade the woman he could love and wanted. Her initial amusement from his attention soon turned into reality, that the man was very different from others she had known. He was impressed by her success, but not awed. She came to understand he was only attracted to the person within her. She knew that no man had ever reached her the way she needed and longed to find one. As she explained to Ava Dale, "Roger makes it possible for me to trust him, to know it's the size of his heart that counts, not what he might own. And, hell, Ava Dale, he knows I'm a person, not like some trophy he gets for his cattle. When he touches me, I feel there's this real live current flowing between us, even a warmth that means so much, so much."

That night after the awards show, it was the part of him that lay just beneath the warm, swirling waters of the hot tub that she needed the most. She required a renewal and was confident her husband was more than up for a revival of sorts himself.

Dropping her robe on a bench beside the tub, she stepped into the water's soothing blackness. She was met by his eager, strong hands, made silky by the warmth of the water. He met her more than halfway to where they were going. One touch of his hands and the feel of his moist lips on her neck erased all lingering doubts of the evening, except for the ones Rhonda the woman felt so strongly at the moment. There was no surrender on either's part. They were two equal partners in their own private game of love. There would be no losers in the battle each sought. And their individual, real life successes meant nothing then. Each was seeing a pinnacle that had to be reached together. Rhonda was no longer just making love songs. She was making love.

Later, when they were back in the softness of their bed,

he realized some of his wife's familiar ghosts had returned. "Something's still haunting those green eyes. I can see it," he observed.

Sitting up immediately in the bed, what troubled her flowed from her as she sat there clutching the award she had claimed just hours before. "Oh, damn, Roger. I don't want you to think this is just another of those times I get crazy. Lord knows I've put you through enough of those, but you're too damned sweet to ever complain. And I love you for that. But sometimes, and this sure as hell is one of them, sometimes I just can't stop the flood of remembering, thinking about everything that's happened to me. Getting to where I am, sustaining me in many ways, and that's the part that's keeping me here, keeping me alive. That's mainly you. And I love you for that, too. But it's all the twists and turns that I've made that make me so damned grateful. And even scared at times. I've taken hits all my life, and each time I grabbed that old bastard 'Trouble,' turned him around by the throat, and shook him for all he was worth. And what fell out of his so-called pockets was all mine.

"Mama always was proud of me. But mostly because of how I stood up for myself. So maybe I was doing it for both of us. Mama and me."

Carefully, she put the award back down on the bedside table and continued. "No, I'm not feeling sorry for myself. I never have. Never. But I do get tired. Nothing's ever been easy. Not a single thing was easy as long as I can remember. And I sure as hell have my limits. All the hit records, all the applause, all the awards on earth are not enough to make up for what it takes to keep your soul alive in this business." She paused, staring at her bare knees, which she was holding with both arms.

Roger said nothing, letting her go on. He could see she was rambling, but he knew it was from her aching heart.

"And I've got a few more hills to climb even after tonight. I just hope you won't get tired of me and how much winning means to this country girl from backwater Alabama. Just stay with me. And I'm going to tell you one more time and then time after time after that that I love you." Turning her head and looking into his eyes, she explained, "For loving me and how proud I am that you're the one true reward for all my work to survive. You're the one I can hang on to and not be afraid I'll regret it."

Tears began to cross her smiling lips. "Maybe I can't make the earth move, but I can say 'Honey, thank you.'" She unwrapped her arms from around her knees and moved slowly to his side of the bed. Reaching for him she said, "Roger, hold me. Never let go. This woman loves you so damn much."

The morning after the awards show, Music Row was the center of activity for all of the fans, at least Rhonda thought so from the size of the crowd. Cars, campers, and dozens of buses were all lined up along the street where several police officers attempted to direct the flow. It was the fans' big opportunity to actually meet the stars.

An acknowledged fan himself, Mayor Brick Webster was present to welcome as many as he could to the party at the Hall of Fame. It was an event dedicated to the wise proposition many music executives voiced, that fans needed to be appreciated. Rhonda Haynes understood that better than anyone.

Roger cautioned her when he heard she was determined to be present for the party. "Babe, you've been under one big strain and you know that. You need a rest. Why don't you just show up, stay a little while, and come on back home?" he suggested.

"Roger," she replied, "you know what these things do for me. Thanks to winning last night, I've got a genuine glow inside and I want to share it."

"I thought that glow might be from something else last night," he winked.

"Sure didn't cool things off. That's for sure," she smiled. "Honey, you know I've never been one of those studio hermits. I can't just put out records and avoid the public because I'm some sort of big shot. I've never been that way and that's a surefire way to cut short a career. Those honest-to-goodness real people out there are important to me. And I sure as hell hope I continue to be important to them."

What she didn't tell him was that she had called Scott Satterfield and asked him to meet her at Athena Records at five o'clock that afternoon, immediately after the party at the Hall of Fame.

She had called Scott early enough to wake him that morning. "And have Dusty there, too, along with the musicians. We'll need him to get that song ready just as quick as he can. I like it, but it needs some work. Hopefully, you two have been working on it."

He assured her they had. "When I called him last night, he had already been reworking some of the lines. I listened and think he's got it right. You'll just have to see." They talked only a few minutes longer and agreed on five o'clock.

Right after lunch she left for Music Row. As Entertainer of the Year, Rhonda held court in a special area under the huge tent on the grounds of the Hall of Fame. She greeted each fan just as if the fan was the actual guest of honor. She wouldn't have it any other way. At about four-thirty the party was still teeming with the crowd for the huge reception honoring all the winners from the night before. Outside the tent, Rhonda stood in a group of Japanese tourists, the tallest barely reaching her shoulders. One at a time each of the Japanese left the group, took a picture, returned to the group for the next shot, and on and on until each had the famous redhead captured in a Nikon. She relished every minute of it, but finally welcomed the chance to go back to the tent and her chair behind the table covered with stacks of photographs and albums to be signed.

There was a long line in front of her table when she sat back down. She instantly picked up one of the felt-tipped pens and asked the young girl who was next in line, "And who's this for?"

The girl replied in a heavy accent, "My name is Emma."

"I'll bet you're from Germany or somewhere like that," Rhonda said. "Do you spell it E-m-m-a?" she inquired.

"Yes, ma'am," the blushing girl responded. "And I would like one for my grandfather. His name is Helmut," she offered as she gestured back to a small group of German tourists who were not standing in line.

Rhonda looked at them and immediately fixed on a tall older man. He looked to be in his late sixties or so and had the reddest hair she had ever seen aside from her own.

"Is that your grandfather? The one with the bright red hair?" she asked. The girl replied that he was, and Rhonda asked her to have him come over to the table. When the elderly gentleman followed his granddaughter to Rhonda's table, she stood up and stuck out her hand. She noted he was a fine-looking man and imagined he had been quite handsome when he was young.

"I've always wanted to meet someone with hair as red as mine," she said as she took his hand warmly into hers. "I had no idea the good Lord made two heads like ours." She laughed, seeing the delighted man blush.

"Thank you," he finally said, speaking in an accent even stronger than his granddaughter's. "We enjoy your music in our country. We are very glad to be here and to meet you. Thank you."

"Well, not half as glad as I am. Here're your photographs. I hope I spelled your name right." She said the name "Helmut" out loud. "I've heard that name before somewhere. But I sign so many autographs it could have been anywhere."

Glancing at the picture, he assured her, "Yes, that is correct. Thank you."

"I'll tell you what. If I ever tour in Germany, be sure to come see me. I'll know you're there. Can't miss that gorgeous hair in any audience," she said, and everyone around the table laughed. The young girl and her grandfather were obviously thrilled.

At that point, Carl came up behind the table and reminded her it was time to meet Scott and the others at the studio. Waving one last time to the crowd as cameras flashed, Rhonda left the reception and followed Carl quickly to the car. The next stop would be Athena Records, five blocks away, where Scott, Dusty, and "Your Lying Arms" were waiting.

CHAPTER 19

Rhonda and her friends had long agreed that by far the best hamburgers in Nashville came from the busy kitchen at Rotier's, a small, hugely popular café near the Vanderbilt University campus on the west side of town. Since 1945 the Rotier family provided some of the best food and hospitality in town to hungry students and Nashville residents. The restaurant's hamburgers won hands down each year in the annual newspaper poll to name the best of this and that. Evelyn Rotier, a long-time fan of Rhonda's, kept an autographed photograph prominently displayed among the glowing signs behind the bar, which only served beer. "You don't need anything stronger or fancier, my friend," the feisty Mrs. Rotier was quick to tell anyone who inquired about a glass of wine or a shot of Jack Daniels' finest.

After leaving the fans' party on Music Row, Rhonda and Carl walked into the studio at Athena Records a few minutes after five o'clock. The first thing she spied was a large sack of hamburgers and onion rings from Rotier's.

"Scott, this has to be your doing. You're a saint and a mind reader to boot," she said and gave him a big hug. "I'm absolutely starved. That puny breakfast this morning didn't come close to making up for last night. And I don't just mean the awards show. You get Roger in that hot tub . . ." she said and laughed, never finishing the sentence.

She was going through the sack of food looking for ketchup packets when Dusty walked into the studio. He was holding a guitar and had been in another part of the building working alone. "Hope you've got one of those for me," he stated, leaning the guitar against an empty stool as he walked over to the small table where the food and soft drinks were.

"No," Rhonda teased, determined to keep the mood light, "writers don't get to eat. You're overpaid as it is. Besides, one of Evelyn's hamburgers might spoil you," she laughed, tossing a slice of pickle into her grinning mouth.

Just as she had requested the night before, Scott and Dusty, along with several musicians, had been at the studio since nine o'clock that morning. Their assignment was to get "Your Lying Arms" into better shape, as she had instructed Scott, "And before I get there at five." No one was quite sure how, but the song was no longer "Loving in Your Lying Arms," but simply "Your Lying Arms." Not even Dusty questioned the change.

On many occasions Rhonda observed the importance of a song's title. "Sometimes that alone is what attracts me to the song in the first place. It's the entire message, down and dirty, pure and simple. It either gets through to you right off the bat or it doesn't." Her instincts told her "Your Lying Arms" was no different.

Anticipating that they had recorded at least a couple of takes for her to hear, she wanted to get right to business. Seeing everyone had their mouths full of food, she tossed her hamburger wrapper into a trashcan and took her place on a stool. "Okay, folks, what kind of dazzle have you got to show me?"

But before the tape could be played, Dusty had something to say. "I worked on it last night while you were at the awards. By the way, congratulations. And you looked like, well, dynamite. I did mange to catch the last hour or so of the show. Hell, you made those models in the commercials look like dog pound rejects."

"Yeah, sure, dreamer. But thanks," she responded, enjoying the flattery all the same. *Same old Dusty,* she thought, *always the charmer.* "Now how about that song?"

Fingering his guitar, Dusty continued to say what was on his mind. "I thought the words were pretty much right as they were, and the phrasing's consistent with what you've done before," he explained. "It was the bridge in the second stanza that needed some fine tuning, no pun intended," making everyone hiss.

Sensing it was time to play show and tell, the technician left the room and entered the control booth as Scott motioned toward the large glass enclosure. "We've got two takes for you to listen to, Rhonda," he explained. "There's just a slight variation where we emphasize different things. You'll see what I mean." With that brief introduction, he again nodded to the technician and the tape was keyed.

Rhonda leaned against the back of her stool with her hands clasped around one knee. Staring first at the floor and then at the lights on the ceiling, she looked at no one while the tape played. Even with just piano, a bass, and Dusty's guitar, she felt what she was hearing was even stronger than she remembered from the first time. Instantly, she knew it was vintage Dusty, and to her it was pure magic. There was no doubt in her mind, or anyone else's in the room. After listening to both versions, she said she wanted to hear the tape again. Scott motioned to the sound booth and within seconds the room was once again filled with Dusty's voice,

Dusty's words delivering the song's intense message. At one point Rhonda glanced over to Carl and saw he wasn't smiling. She preferred not to think about what was probably on his protective mind at that moment.

When the tape stopped for the second time, Rhonda finally straightened out her legs and stood up. "I must say, you fellas sure know how to hit a girl right where it counts. That's one nice day's work there." Looking at Dusty for the first time since hearing the tape, she admitted, "And a few long nights for you I'm sure." Taking in everyone's pleased, even relieved expressions, she added, "Right now, I'm not sure which version I like best."

Before anyone could offer his or her opinion, she outlined the strategy she wanted to follow. "Scott, I don't think that has to be decided today, right now anyway. Let's schedule a session for as soon as you and Avery can get everyone together. I'll do both versions, maybe add a twist of my own, and then we'll decide. But I want to get on it as soon as you can make the arrangements."

"Sounds perfect." The voice was Avery Springer's. He had entered the room just as the tape concluded for the second time, preferring to listen in his office alone, without distractions and without anyone being aware of his critical presence. In his office he had listened with a broad smile on his face. "How does Friday sound to everyone?" he proposed and walked across the room and stood behind Rhonda, gently rubbing her shoulders with both hands.

"Only if you keep doing that until then, big boy," his star purred approvingly. Rhonda thrived on attention, but, more importantly appreciated Avery's ability to anticipate her personal concerns about her career needs and his willingness to meet those needs, one being a monster hit song at that particular moment.

"Then five o'clock Friday it is," Avery announced. "Everyone keep your schedules open."

When the designated day and hour arrived, Rhonda's adrenaline was flowing. She was glowing from expectations of what she could actually do with what she considered Dusty's best work in years. But as she had explained to Ava Dale on the telephone the night before, "The business is changing. It's more than just who you know. A singer's got to have a broader appeal to more than just folks who love country music. The real money's in having a total package, one that can sell in other markets." And she was right.

The traditional good-old-boy network, long the engine driving country music, had been replaced by skilled businessmen and public relations experts. The business had weathered the years of abuse and mishandling by the Al Wendells of their world who "gave leeches a bad name," as she once described him to Ava Dale. That ilk had been replaced just as the red shag carpet and black naugahyde sofas in the offices had been replaced by Oriental rugs and fine English antiques. Dubious handshake deals were also a thing of the past. They were replaced by contracts thicker than a telephone directory in Manhattan, where most of them originated.

Within that environment, success was no accident. That valuable commodity was carefully calculated, even manipulated to perfection. It was also a world in which the artist was most definitely not the only player in the drama. The bottom line was survival, as dictated by the financial balance sheet, and depended heavily on the songwriters, who in the past were often overlooked, but left parts of their souls on a piece of paper. Dusty was no different. He once told Rhonda, "I sell pieces of myself for another person's feast."

He had been doing it for years. He had talent, knew words, but equally important was his strong sense of what would sell in the changing music marketplace. While he gave of a precious commodity within himself, Dusty was first and foremost, however, a taker. Rhonda was witness to there never being a time he wouldn't take all that he could from anyone he could. His songwriting skills never overwhelmed his inability to control his greed and selfish indulgences. Rhonda once told Ava Dale, "When it comes to getting down to the clinches, Dusty's got four hands. I learned that the hard way."

Rhonda had loved him as a husband, cherished his talent as a writer, but she had also come to despise the side of him that left her anything but comfortable where Dusty was concerned. "There's part of me he must still have a hold on, Ava Dale," she admitted, "but I'll never trust him again with the rest of me."

But where her career was concerned and her compelling need for a hit record, she feared she had to rely on Dusty, at least his words. For that reason she was willing to let him back into that part of her world, but only so far. She was cautious where he was involved, ever mindful of the line from the only song she had both written and recorded—"This hurt's taken on a life of its own."

When Friday came, with Carl's assistance Rhonda was right on time at the studio. As Avery had insisted, everyone knew to give that date a top priority and knew they were committed to stay until the boss said it was time to go. Avery told the switchboard operator to stay as long as they did and only take messages. There were to be no calls passed along to anyone "aside from a death in the family or something of that nature." Rarely was Avery so authoritative, but when it was something as important as that session was to Rhonda, he pulled no punches. It was business, first and foremost.

Rhonda also realized what it took to get the best from the people around her. While some big names showed up at recording sessions looking like last week's meatloaf wearing farm clothes, hair in a wad, and in need of a shower, Rhonda knew better. That day every hair was in place. Her tight fitting jeans were topped by a black leather belt with a huge turquoise buckle and a soft, flowing white peasant blouse with ruffles on the cuffs. It was one way she showed how much she appreciated the talent and loyalty around her and how much they meant to her. Looking good was one of her passions.

Once in the studio, she immediately took a mental roll call. The entire crew was there, even Dusty, who was rarely on time. First, she gave Avery a warm hug, and then it was down to business. "All right," the producer began as Rhonda settled onto her customary stool before the microphone. "Let's get this thing going. First, I want Rhonda to listen once to just the music, no words, if that's okay with you." Shifting her position on the stool, she nodded her approval. He continued with the plan. "Then we'll just walk through this a few times with Rhonda doing whatever she wants with it. You all listen to her interpretation. Make your adjustments, but don't go too far from what's already on the page, at least this first time. Any major changes we'll want to discuss at length."

The session lasted almost two hours. Rhonda told them she was extremely comfortable with what she heard and the lyrics were superb as written. That made it all very easy for the professionals they were. Dusty had fine-tuned every phrase just to her liking, as only he could. After four complete run-throughs with musicians and lyrics, Avery suggested a break. "You folks take a rest. We've done all that seems needed. We're all tired, although Rhonda seems to be as fresh as when she got here," he observed, aware her adrenaline had never ceased to pump. Taking their cue from the producer, everyone left the room with instructions to reassemble in fifteen minutes.

Realizing she had forgotten her purse, Rhonda returned to the sound room after a quick trip to the ladies room. She walked over to where her purse was, initially thinking no one else was there. Then she noticed Dusty was sitting quietly in one corner, leaning back against the wall with his eyes closed. She thought he must have been sleeping, so she started to go through her purse looking for something for her growing headache as quietly as she could.

Before she realized he had even moved, Dusty was standing beside her. She was startled at first, then saw the look in his eyes. She was immediately afraid of what was there. Somehow between the time everyone left the room and when she returned, Dusty had taken a hit of something, probably cocaine. There was no mistaking it from what she saw in his expression. She had seen that look too many times and despised it. She had long ago acknowledged Dusty was enough of a load when he was straight. "He is more than I care to ever put up with again," she once admitted to Ava Dale.

"Well, what did you think?" he asked, watching her take her headache tablet from her purse.

She calmly straightened up, but didn't retreat a step. She told herself not to overreact, just keep it friendly. After all, she reasoned, there are eight other people here and that reassured her, knowing they were due back any minute.

"If you have to ask, you've lost your touch," she replied, at first defiant. "I think the second time I went through it, there was near perfection for sure. Everyone, everything just clicked. Surely, you heard it. At that point I really felt I could convey what the words were saying. I just hope I did them justice," she said, actually hoping the flattery would not be missed and would, perhaps, placate him, maybe even alleviate any anxiety he might be feeling about his work.

"Hell, Rhonda, you had that damn meaning nailed down from the very beginning," he protested, a bit too strongly due to the rush of the cocaine. "Don't give me that shit. You're a pro. You know what you're doing," he said. "You always know what you're doing. You always have. Always," he emphasized, and she detected some resentment. Something she had heard before.

He placed his hand on her shoulder, making her fear of him even more real. *Or*, she wondered, *was it actually disgust that he could be so stupid, so damn self-destructive?* Before she could decide, Dusty's mouth was on hers. With both his arms clasped behind her, he held her close and sought to probe her closed mouth with his hardened tongue. In only an instant, it was over. Getting no response from her, he released her. She stepped back and bumped the music stand, sending some of the sheet music flying.

"What's the matter, Rhonda?" he asked sarcastically. "Forgotten how it feels?" Before she knew what she was doing and before he could do anything else, she grabbed a handful of sheet music and slapped him across the face, then let the paper fall as he drew back, expecting a second blow.

"Don't you doubt for one damn minute I've forgotten anything, you simple son of a bitch," she said in a low, snarling voice. "How could I?" she demanded. "Every time you're near me you remind me of what a grasping asshole you are and what a fool I was to ever, ever think you were anything but that."

Recovering from her blow, Dusty snapped, "Hell, I've given—"

"Given my foot," she interrupted. "For everything you've ever given, you took a thousand times more. Don't give me that innocent crap. Sure, Dusty, at one time I even loved you. You can bet your sweet ass on that one. But then you made choices a long time ago, and you made all the wrong ones. Every goddamn one of them, and all by yourself. Don't you ever think about blaming me for what's happened to you. And don't blame anything else that happened before I met you. A lot of people have rough things happen to them when they're growing up. I sure as hell did and you know it. But, dammit, people with any backbone at all get beyond the crap and go on. But you made all the wrong choices, and long before you met me. Every goddamn one of them you made all by yourself. Don't blame me for your mess. You did it all and for what? Your damn drugs? That seems to be all you really care about, maybe ever did." She paused only to get her breath. "The feelings I had for you are history, mister. You stomped all over those feelings a long time ago, so now you listen and listen good," she warned him. Her fear had been replaced by rage. "If working with you is impossible for me, then that's the way it'll just have to be. Period. That's for you to think about and for me to decide. Sure, I like your work. I dearly love what you do with words. This song's the best thing you've probably ever done, and it might work out to be the same for me. But crap like what you just pulled is not a price I'm willing to pay. Understand?"

Not waiting for him to answer, she hammered home her point. "Now the rest of them will be walking back in here any minute now. One word from me, one little hint about this, and you'll be out that door so fast your sorry head will be spinning even worse that it already probably is. Either you tell me right now this will never happen again or I'll have your butt bounced from every studio in this town. Pull another stunt like this and the closest you'll ever get to music again will be cleaning toilets at truck stops in Branson, Missouri."

There was only silence from him. Stoned silence. Rhonda thought she saw a tear in his eye, but wasn't sure. Suddenly the silence was broken when the door opened and all the others entered in the middle of a heated discussion about a picture of Okalene Harris in a recent *People* magazine article. The debate was whether "Old Okie's boobs," as Scott phrased it, seemed larger than the last time they had seen her in her most recent late night television interview.

Nothing was ever said about the incident with Dusty at the studio. Rhonda knew she didn't have to tell anyone. She had told Dusty, and she was confident that was enough. For once she felt he fully understood she meant every word she had said, every threat she had made and knew she would keep. He also understood why.

CHAPTER 20

"That was Grady Garland and his new hit single, 'Taking My Time This Time,' and I'm Sonny Boyd Everette here at FM one-o-eight in beautiful Music City, U.S.A., where it's a typical summer day. No surprise we've got country music fans from all over the world making the rounds on Music Row and out at Opryland. Enjoying all the terrific things you'd expect to find in the country music capital of the entire world. I caught a really great evening last night at the Bluebird Café, and it was standing room only. It was song-writers' night and some of the best in the business were seat-ed in the round and giving the audience quite a show. You folks don't want to miss that one while you're in town. Now here's one song I'm sure you've been waiting to hear all morning. It's without a doubt the fastest rising song in many years. It's only been out for a few days, and it's obviously heading straight for the number one spot. Here's 'Your Lying Arms' from everyone's Entertainer of the Year, the fabulous Rhonda Haynes."

When the call came, Avery Springer was glad he was sit-ting down. It was a late Thursday afternoon. His attorney had just left the music producer's office at Athena, but not without giving his client a large stack of contracts the attorney said, "need to be back on my desk by the first of the week and no later." Avery understood that meant the lawyer himself had used up all the extra time and the client had to haul ass. *Who's working for whom?* Avery wondered to himself as the attorney departed, probably on his way to a golf course.

Before the door could shut behind the lawyer, Avery's long-time secretary, Vicki Wright, entered the room, only to find her boss heading for the wet bar and a second scotch and water. "Avery, I need to leave," she said, "if it's all right. My son forgot to pick up his tux for the prom tonight, and now I have to get to the rental store before it closes. Honestly, Jason's never given me a minute's trouble. But sometimes I wonder how he ties his own shoes."

"Sure, Vicki," he replied. "Go ahead. Is anyone else still here?" he asked.

"No, everyone left over an hour ago. I've forwarded the phones in here so you can hear it if anyone calls. They rarely do this time of the day, especially in the summer. Even those jerks with car phones stuck in their ears are usually too tired by now to use them, unless they need to reserve a tennis court at their club," she assured him. "See you tomorrow. Don't forget you have an appointment with Rick Douglass at ten o'clock tomorrow morning. The rest of the day looks pretty clear so far."

With that she left, leaving the door to his office ajar. He knew she would test the locks on both outside doors before leaving, but then she was back. "I checked the doors. Everything's locked. Don't forget to set the alarm system when you leave," she advised.

Not waiting for his reply, she vanished again.

Placing his glass on the note pad, Avery leaned forward and reluctantly picked up the receiver on the third ring. It was several minutes after his secretary had gone and he was enjoying the rare quiet. "This is Avery Springer," he said, unaccustomed to not being told first who was on the other end of the line before taking a call.

The operator said the call was from the White House and asked him to hold for a Mr. Ronald Haroldson, who promptly came on the line. "Mr. Springer, this is Ron Haroldson. I'm calling for the White House on behalf of President Bennett. How are you this evening?"

Sitting up a little straighter in his leather chair, the record executive looked down at the telephone set and replied, "I'm fine. Thank you."

"I am sorry to bother you this late in the day," the caller began, as if he thought everyone in Nashville crawled into a cave at sundown, and it was not even that late yet. "But I need to discuss a possible personal appearance by your client, Rhonda Haynes. We checked with Senator Robinson, and he assured us you are the proper person to contact about this."

"Oh, yes, the Senator knows his constituency very well," Avery assured him. What he did not say was that in his opinion and many other's Senator Reed Robinson was a dull-witted pretty boy whose only real interest was expanding his constituency to include all of America by claiming the White House for himself one day.

"Let me explain," Haroldson offered.

"Please do, Mr. Haroldson. You certainly have my undivided attention."

The apparently young and very authoritative presidential assistant was eager to oblige. "President and Mrs. Bennett will be hosting a formal dinner in four weeks for the visiting Prime Minister of New Zealand and his wife. The White House recently learned the Prime Minister is a big fan of country music. We are hoping to have Miss Haynes perform in the East Room after the state dinner."Without waiting for Avery to respond, he further explained the call. "The President is a long-time fan of Miss Haynes. He and the First Lady were thrilled when she won her recent Entertainer of the Year award. She's always been one of their favorites. And, yes, they did watch the awards ceremony. Miss Haynes is a class act, and they both know Prime Minister Wilkins would be impressed to see her perform in person. Her work is no stranger to New Zealand," he stated in a very reassuring tone.

Moving the receiver from his face, Avery quickly took a sip from his Scotch and carefully returned the glass to the note pad. "Of course, Mr. Haroldson," he began. "This is quite a surprise, I must say. And certainly an honor goes without saying. I believe you said the date is August eighth, is that right?"

"Yes, the evening of August eight. Miss Haynes and her party would have to be in Washington on the seventh to check out the logistics in the East Room. We will make all the necessary arrangements for the trip working in conjunction with your office, of course. Naturally, everything will have to be checked out before the performance, and she probably would prefer to have at least one opportunity to rehearse before the actual event itself. And everyone accompanying her would have to be cleared for security. That's standard practice. You understand."

"I understand fully. Yes, that will be undoubtedly be no problem. I've known Rhonda and everyone in her band for several years. Other than a few parking tickets, each one can be vouched for, I assure you."

"Nevertheless, as you might expect, we have our procedures for such matters. We will make sure everything is as painless as possible."

"Well, Mr. Haroldson, I—" Avery began.

Before he could finish his thought, the White House events coordinator was way ahead of him. "Even though you are her producer and manager, we understand you will want to confirm all this with Miss Haynes. Do you think you could have an answer by tomorrow about this time?" Haroldson asked.

"You're correct about that. Several schedules will have to be checked. But I can assure you that, pending any unforeseen contractual or scheduling problems I don't know about, I'm confident Rhonda will be honored to accept the President's kind invitation. He's very gracious."

"Then I will expect to hear from you tomorrow. We can work out further specifics at that time," Haroldson said. And with an exchange of telephone and facsimile numbers, the conversation ended.

With his drink firmly in hand, Avery sat back in his chair and smiled the smile of someone who had just won the lottery. The respect his client would enjoy, not to mention himself, he admitted, was immeasurable. A command performance at the White House before heads of state and the Washington in-crowd was quite an honor. A coup in anyone's book.

"Chuck Kaiser, eat your fucking heart out," he said aloud to the empty office. Then he leaned further back in his chair and laughed the laugh of a very satisfied man.

"Rhonda's down at the stables, Avery, looking at the new mare she bought at the auction in Kentucky last week." Roger had answered the telephone at Honeysuckle Haven. He was expecting an important call himself. "Everybody seems to have decided to take the day off around here. So it's just Rhonda and me holding down the fort. She's down there with the veterinarian. Is there something I can tell her or can she call you back?" he asked.

"Well, Roger, this is one call she needs right now," Avery said confidently. "Don't worry. It's the kind of news she'll like. Both of you will, in fact."

"Tell you what, Avery. Let's hang up. Then you call back. I'll switch the phones so the call will ring down there at the stables. Just let it ring a few times longer than normal. She'll answer, I'm sure."

"And, Roger, after she answers, why don't you pick up and listen? This will be too good to miss. That I promise, my friend."

Just as her husband said, Rhonda was down at the white brick horse stables about a quarter of a mile from the main house. She was with the veterinarian who had accompanied her the previous week to the thoroughbred horse auction at Keeneland in Kentucky. She had purchased a two-year-old mare whose sire was a Kentucky Derby winner. The horse had arrived at Honeysuckle Haven the previous afternoon in the special horse carrier her new owner had also acquired at the auction. Sorrel with a flash of white down her forehead to her nose, the mare was the latest example of Rhonda's favorite and most extravagant way of enjoying the benefits of her success. She loved her horses and spared no expense in their upkeep and training. A veterinarian on call and stables as spotless as a hospital kitchen were just some of the indulgences she gave to her very expensive hobby. A treasured tourist photograph was of Rhonda riding one of her thoroughbreds or walking horses down to the front gate of Honeysuckle Haven to wave at the tour buses.

"I earn it and by damn I'll spend it any way I please.

These gorgeous critters are my family, some of the best friends I have, other than you, Ava Dale," she often said. She had driven her red Jeep Grand Cherokee down to the stables by herself. All the lights were on inside the building. She was just sitting on the brick floor across the walkway at the stall in which the new mare was standing and staring right back at her proud owner. The animal's official name was Razzle Dazzle, but Rhonda was trying to come up with a pet name for her, when Dr. John Lynch walked into the stables carrying his small black case.

Rising from her comfortable position, she asked, "John, don't you think she's even prettier than you remember? Just look at those black eyes and those lashes. Have you ever seen such a glint in your life?"

"Sorry to be late, and you're right. There's no doubt about it, Rhonda. This mare's a real jewel. Looks like she made the trip okay, too," he gladly observed as he walked to the stall and began rubbing the horse's slender, elegant nose.

"Well, that should be no real surprise. I may take that carrier on the road and ride in it myself. Beats that tour bus I've got now," she laughed. "Think I'll call her Charo," she stated pensively. "She's got a certain bounce in her when she walks."

"Maybe you can train her to *cuchi cuchi*," he said, and they both laughed at the prospect.

Rhonda motioned to the stable hand who had been standing nearby. "Tommy, take the new mare out to the holding area. The light's better there. John can check her out better out there." The veterinarian had briefly examined the horse at the auction, but Rhonda wanted a more thorough examination now that her Charo was home.

The stable worker was almost out of the stable door when the telephone rang.

Realizing Roger was forwarding her calls, Rhonda told them, "Go ahead with the horse while I answer the phone." It was ringing in the small office at the other end of the building. "Let me get that, John," she said. "I won't be too long."

Entering the office, Rhonda didn't take time to sit down. She remained standing with one knee in the tapestry chair beside the old oak desk and reached for the telephone receiver. "Yes," she said, indicating her impatience with whatever was providing the interruption. She immediately recognized Avery's voice and detected an unusual excitement.

"Sorry to bother you, Rhonda, but I asked Roger to send this call down to you. I don't think this should wait," he began. "I've asked Roger to pick up. Roger, are you there?"

"I'm right here," her husband replied. "Can't wait to hear this one."

Avery continued, "I wanted you both to hear this at the same time. Rhonda, I sure hope you're sitting down."

"Well, I wasn't, but I am now," she responded. She finally gave in and reclined in the chair. "What's got you so fired up, Avery? Roger's right. This must be really off the wall."

"I just hung up from talking with a big fan of yours, Rhonda. Well, actually it was a representative of his, but he's a big fan regardless. Really big," he remarked.

"Now don't tell me Whacker Rawlins is in town," she said sarcastically.

"No, not your favorite mayor." Avery had to laugh at her guess. "Try the President of the United States. Martin Bennett himself. President Martin Bennett," he repeated slowly for emphasis.

"I'll be damned," was Roger's response.

"What's this all about, Avery?" Rhonda asked. "Are you sure someone wasn't pulling a fast one on you? Tom Collins just loves playing jokes. Sounds to me like something he might do." Collins, a prominent record producer on Music Row, had once sent Okalene Harris a milking machine with a note saying "Thinking of you."

"No, it wasn't my friend Tom." Leaning forward to check his notes, he gave them the details. "His name, the guy who called, is Ron Haroldson. He's President Bennett's appointment secretary or something. Anyway, the Prime Minister of New Zealand is making an official visit to the White House. They want you to entertain after the big state dinner. Seems the Prime Minister is a bona fide fan of country music. You're to provide the nice gentleman with the evening's finale."

There was a long silence in the stable office. No one else said anything. At the studio Avery took a sip of his drink. At the main house Roger sat quietly waiting for his wife to respond. Rhonda was staring at the trophies and prize ribbons lining the stable office walls. Since it was getting dark, she reached forward and turned on the large brass lamp on the desk. The light caught the shiny trophies, making each one cast a tiny reflection of light on the reigning queen of the world country music, a world that suddenly reached to the other side of the globe.

After Avery's news had been absorbed, she finally made a comment. "Hell, Avery, I don't even know where New Zealand is," she exaggerated. "But I sure as hell think we can find the White House. The rest will be up to you fellows to figure out."

"No, Miss Rhonda, it will, as always, be up to you. We'll just tag along. It should be quite a show. It's a great honor, but nothing you can't handle and don't deserve, my friend," he stated sincerely. "What do you think?"

"What I think is that this is going to be a night for all of

us to remember for a long, long time," she said softly, somewhat overwhelmed. "That's exactly what I'm going to try to
deliver, one great memory for all of us."

Roger broke into the conversation. "Does this mean I
should crank up the hot tub?"

"Not tonight, Mr. One-track Mind," she laughed. "I
meant the night of the performance in Washington. But
don't drain the damn thing either any time soon."

"Okay," Avery said. "I've kept you from your new mare
long enough. The evening in Washington is August the
eighth. The guy who called said he would get back to me
tomorrow with more details. What say we all get together in
my office at the studio Monday and get started on this
thing?" he suggested. "There will be a million things to consider. We may as well get started on the list. We don't have a
lot of time to waste."

Rhonda agreed and asked Roger to call Carl to make
sure he would be available to drive her to Nashville on
Monday. After everyone hung up, Rhonda sat in the chair a
moment longer reflecting on the call.

Speaking to no one, she said, "From little old Darden all
the way to the White House. Quite a trip for a housekeep-
er's skinny little girl." Rising from the chair, she turned off
the lamp. In almost total darkness she added, "Mama, I know
you'll be right there with me. You always have been. I love
you."

CHAPTER 21

The members of Rhonda's band, the technicians, and the three back-up singers all took the same American Airlines flight to Washington early on August 7, the day before the scheduled performance at 1600 Pennsylvania Avenue. There were five musicians, two technicians, and a road manager whose job it was to "make damn sure everyone and all the equipment get to the right place at the right time and sober," their boss had ordered. Everyone was booked into the Washington Hilton near the White House, as arranged by the President's events coordinator.

At the hotel a large ballroom was reserved for two scheduled rehearsals, one on the seventh and one on the eighth. Avery arranged a private Lear jet to take Rhonda and Roger, Ruth Staggs, his wife, and himself to the capital. "I don't want you to have to spend any time going through National Airport. There are third world countries with better facilities than that," he explained to Rhonda when they were going over the details for the trip. The Lear landed at a private terminal in nearby Bethesda, Maryland, where a limousine waited to take them to the Hilton. Avery wanted everything to be as free of hassles as possible and meticulously planned every minute from when Rhonda left Honeysuckle Haven until she returned.

One glitch did occur, but Avery admitted, "Truthfully no one was too upset." Dusty failed to pass the security clearance because of his arrest for cocaine possession a few years before. The White House felt strongly about having him as part of an evening with a President as prominent in the fight against drugs as Martin Bennett was. Although Rhonda knew Dusty was disappointed he couldn't make the trip, especially since he had arranged a special medley for the performance, she was actually relieved he wouldn't be along and risk causing a problem.

The week before, Rhonda and Ruth spent hours deciding on just the right look for the performance. The dress they eventually chose was a full one hundred and eighty degrees from what she wore to the awards show. As Entertainer of the Year that night she wanted to dazzle her fans and succeeded wildly, everyone agreed. The fan magazines were still talking about the emerald green outfit, the white feather boa, and the hair treatment that "made a raging forest fire look tame" one writer said. Rhonda wanted something different for the East Room. "In my way of thinking this requires definite class, not brass," she stated to Ruth over coffee in her bedroom suite. And class it was.

She chose a floor-length skirt, a cascade of soft, black moiré ruffles, and a long sleeve, white silk blouse with a scoop neckline. "And, of course, I've got to wear Roger's emerald necklace and earrings. They'll look fabulous and, besides, he'd kill me if I didn't," she giggled. Ruth had suggested a pearl choker, but Rhonda was adamant about the emeralds. "The outfit is subtle enough, Ruth. Let's give them just a little flash," she said. "Those emeralds should do the trick very nicely."

As a back-up they agreed to take the white sequined dress she wore two years before to a convention of record executives meeting in Nashville. That occasion was the last time she had seen Chuck Kaiser anywhere. The word on Music Row was that Kaiser had been given "early retirement" from his position at Sun Spot Records. To many in the music business, Kaiser's leaving Nashville was good news and long overdue. For that reason alone Rhonda had fond memories of that dress. But it was not as much a matter of being superstitious, as being prone to go with her excellent instincts about her looks.

Within two hours of reaching the Hilton, the entire Haynes entourage was set up in the hotel ballroom, the Cherry Blossom Room, and waiting for Rhonda to arrive. The first rehearsal was scheduled for the evening of the seventh at eight o'clock with another for the next morning at ten. "We will all go to the White House at two o'clock that afternoon and set up for the performance that night," Avery explained. "And I don't have to tell any of you about the famous East Room and how important all of this is, so act like you're in church, dammit." Rhonda snickered when Avery reminded them about the history of the East Room and all the important celebrities who had entertained there. She always got a kick telling about the time The Captain and Tennille performed before the Queen of England and sang a song about "two muskrats screwing," a story always guaranteed to send Ava Dale into fits of laughter.

A few minutes before eight o'clock the doors to the Cherry Blossom room swung open and in walked the main attraction. Rhonda was glad to see everyone, but wasted little time with small talk. "Listen, folks, we've got only two shots at this," she reminded them, as Avery took a seat in the back of the room. "We've been in tighter spots before, but not quite as fancy, I have to admit. Thank God we don't have to eat with those people tomorrow night and make nice," she said. "Hell, I still don't know where New Zealand is," she lied, but wanted to lighten the mood as best she knew how.

"They raise a lot sheep there," one of the musicians called out.

"Bound for you to know that, Earl. We've all heard those stories about you farm boys and sheep," she teased and everyone roared. Red-faced, Earl was recently divorced and taking a lot of ribbing about his sudden late night escapades.

Still in an organizing frame of mind, she continued, "About the only thing we haven't done before at all, at least not the way it's been arranged this time, is the medley version of some of the songs. It's somewhat different this way. Why don't we run through it first, just to see how it all works together? Then we'll do the entire set from the beginning and finish with 'Your Lying Arms.'" She and Avery had earlier agreed to conclude with the current number one song on the charts. It was the biggest hit single Rhonda had ever had. The smash success of "Your Lying Arms" had exceeded her wildest expectations.

"And the White House did make a specific request that you sing it," Avery reminded her.

The rehearsal lasted until almost ten o'clock that night. At that point Avery, waving his arms for silence, decided that was enough. "I think we all need to get some rest now. And be damn sure to set your watches ahead an hour. Nashville's on Central time, Washington, Eastern. And leave a wake up call with the hotel operator just to be safe," he advised. "We'll all be back in this room at ten tomorrow morning," he instructed.

"I'll have coffee, juice, and Danish for those who prefer to sleep rather than find a real breakfast. Besides, I doubt if you could find country ham and grits on any menu in this town. At least since Jimmy Carter left," she added as everyone headed for the elevators.

When Rhonda and Roger returned to their suite on the seventh floor, they found a special table set up in the living room. On the table the hotel staff placed numerous items and messages that had arrived while Rhonda was rehearsing. "Oh, Roger, look," she gasped, pointing at a large basket of fruit and Godiva chocolates. "The card says 'President and Mrs. Martin Bennett.' Now that's impressive." There was a smaller fruit basket from Garland Parks, president of the Country Music Association in Nashville. Two bottles of champagne, one from Carl Sutton, who stayed home to look after things at Honeysuckle Haven, and the other from Mayor Brick Webster. On a large silver tray, the hotel staff placed several messages and telegrams. There was a note from Dusty, but Roger saw it first and stuck it in his pocket before Rhonda could see it, just to be careful, he assured himself. He would decide later whether to ever let her read it.

CHAPTER 22

The morning newspapers in the nation's capital on the eighth of August were filled with the usual Washington stories. Congress was still debating the budget, and the latest congressman was trying to deny allegations of sexual escapades, that time it was sexual harassment of a prominent senator's personal secretary. Another featured story pertained to the visitor from New Zealand and his importance to the United States' policy toward the Pacific Rim nations. *The Washington Post* carried a front-page story on the arrival of New Zealand's Prime Minister at Dulles International Airport the day before. Prime Minister Harold Wilkins and his wife, Evelyn, were shown with President and Mrs. Bennett warmly receiving them on the White House lawn before the press corps. Wilkins was a particularly important state visitor for the Bennett administration. Its primary objective was to align New Zealand behind the United States' effort to defeat the radical insurgents threatening the elected governments in the Philippines and Malaysia. Australia, Great Britain, and Japan had each been enlisted in President Bennett's determination to maintain stability in the region. New Zealand's support, primarily symbolic, was considered to be crucial in presenting a united front against those groups of former communists who had become radicals with little or no philosophical bent. The danger, as viewed by many Washington insiders, was the threat to vital trade in the Pacific Rim where American business interests were increasingly turning their attention, as well as the administration's own concern for political stability in the area.

At the end of the story about Prime Minster Wilkins, the article contained a few lines about the formal state dinner for the evening of the eighth to be followed by entertainment provided by "country music diva" Rhonda Haynes in the East Room of the White House. Ruth Staggs didn't have to be reminded to clip all such stories for Rhonda's collection of scrapbooks.

"Ruth, I don't know what I'd do without you." Rhonda was expressing a familiar sentiment as she began to get dressed for the performance at the White House. "The morning rehearsal went just fine, and that medley is a winner. Dusty really did some great work on that," she reported. It was the first time his name had been mentioned by anyone during the trip. "And the set-up at the White House went off without a hitch." Ruth had stayed behind to arrange the clothes and accessories when the group went to check out the East Room. "And Kathryn Bennett is one of the nicest people I've ever met."

The President's wife stuck her head in the door of the East Room when Rhonda's people were setting up. "I just had to see how things were going for you," the First Lady explained. She was followed by her ever-present bearded collie, Rowdy, when she strolled into the room and immediately gave Rhonda a warm hug and shook hands with everyone present. "Martin and I are so pleased you could all be here tonight. It's seldom we get to hear anyone so dear to our musical hearts in this place," Mrs. Bennett said, looking at Rhonda. "My daughter just gave me a tape of your new album. It's upstairs in the family quarters. At least I hope it is. I'll have to fight to keep my grandkids from taking it home with them. I told them to buy their own. That should help sales," she added and winked. "But I'm sure you don't need any assistance from me in that department."

"Well, Mrs. Bennett—" Rhonda began and was immediately cut off.

"It's Kathryn to you. All of you," the First Lady insisted.

"Okay, Kathryn," Rhonda smiled, "but you must know how thrilled we are to be here. In my wildest dreams I never thought we would be here in this wonderful place."

"*Your* wildest dreams? Do you think when I married Martin I thought I would be here myself?" They all enjoyed the gracious woman's sense of humor and understood why she was so well loved. She made them feel at home, and with that mission accomplished the President's wife excused herself, after again assuring them how much she and her husband were looking forward to the evening's "main event," as she described it.

The nighttime did not bring an end to the loud traffic, which only added to Rhonda's butterflies. The clock by the king-sized bed showed seven-thirty and the performance of her life was set to begin promptly at ten. Ruth was busy laying out everything Rhonda would wear, while Rhonda sat in front of a large mirror pushing her hair first one way and then another, trying to decide how it would be worn that night.

"I swear, Ruth, before these things, I'm all thumbs. And Roger's no help. He's all thumbs all the time," she remarked. "But I've got you to keep me from flipping out. Thank God for that."

Ruth turned and laughed. "I doubt there's any real chance of you flipping out over anything, even this. I've seen you handle too many tight situations. It'll take more than some prime minister and a bunch of politicians at the White House to rattle you, girl. Why, those people over there are probably nervous because you're coming over. Honey, you are royalty and don't forget it."

Rhonda was still fussing with her hair when the telephone rang. She and Roger, who was in the living room, both picked up at the same time. But before she could speak, her husband said, "Hello." On the other end of the line, Avery quickly asked, "Where's Rhonda?" Curious about his tone of voice, she decided to say nothing for the moment.

"She's in the bedroom with Ruth getting dressed. Is there a problem?" Roger responded, also picking up on the concern in Avery's words.

"I'll tell you, but for Christ's sake, do not tell her," Avery warned.

"Tell her what?"

"Dusty's been killed in a car wreck in Nashville. Carl Sutton heard about it and called me immediately. They found his car wrapped around a utility pole on Briley Parkway. From what they can find out, he was blind running drunk, and Lord knows what else he had in his system this time."

"Damn," Roger groaned. "I hate to say it, but that twerp could have picked a better time to pull a fool stunt like that. Hell, Rhonda doesn't need a jolt like that, particularly tonight. Shit."

"Roger, you've got to make sure no one tells her. I'm calling everyone who's up here with us. They'll keep quiet. Just don't let her take any telephone calls. Some damn reporter from Nashville might try to talk to her. Keep her busy and away from the phone," Avery ordered.

"I will," Roger promised. "Shit," he repeated. "I'll talk with you later. I'll take care of things here."

When her husband and Avery hung up, Rhonda quietly replaced the receiver on the telephone in the bedroom and was confident Ruth never noticed she was on the telephone. Without saying anything to her friend, Rhonda went directly into the bathroom and closed the door. Her cosmetics case was on the counter near the double lavatory. She began rummaging through the case, quickly pushing everything from one side to the other. When she found the small medicine case, she fumbled with the lid. Finally, one tablet rolled into her shaking palm. Looking into the mirror, she saw no tears, only fear. But of what, she wasn't certain. Slowly she leaned against the lavatory countertop and folded her arms, still clutching the mild tranquilizer in her hand. For several minutes she let the water run to make Ruth think she was doing something other than what she was. *I can't let Dusty do this to me again,* was her next thought. *I can't let this get to me, not now, not ever,* she told herself. She realized she had to block out all she had just heard. Dusty Harmon had disrupted her life too many times. Those occasions were painful to recall, but they were part of the past and had to stay there. She wanted to convince herself Dusty's death wouldn't affect her, but she was afraid that wasn't possible. Looking into the mirror, she spoke to her reflection, "But I've got to try. And on my own."

Still holding the tranquilizer, she walked to the toilet, tossed the tablet into the bowl, and gently flushed it. Opening the bathroom door, Rhonda walked back into the bedroom and again sat down in front of the dresser. "What do you think?" she asked Ruth, then pushed her hair into a pile on top of her head. "Let's get this thing in gear, my friend."

CHAPTER 23

"Thank you. Thank you so much. And good evening, President Bennett, Mrs. Bennett, Prime Minister and Mrs. Wilkins, ladies and gentlemen. Thank you for such a gracious welcome. Oh my, this is such an honor for all of us."

There she was. Rhonda Haynes. Standing before the nation's First Family, foreign dignitaries, and Washington's elite. And she loved it. She was the picture of elegance and was determined to charm her exclusive audience. Her warm expression of gratitude over with, she knew right where to start her courtship of every heart beating in the room before her.

"Mrs. Bennett," she began. She couldn't bring herself to say Kathryn before all those people. "You made us feel so at home earlier today. My first song is, I am told, one of your favorites. You see we have sources, too," she said, and the audience appreciated the humor. "It was written by Cole Porter who, I think it would be safe to say, probably didn't have a country girl from Alabama in mind at the time." Everyone again laughed softly in anticipation. Then with the first note of "I've Got You Under My Skin" Rhonda took control of the room and never relinquished it, not for a single moment. Every song, especially the medley of four of her greatest hits, was well received. A smile never left the face of Prime Minister Wilkins, who held his wife's hand throughout the performance, letting go only to applaud vigorously.

She completed the medley and acknowledged the enthusiastic response of her obviously delighted audience. "Finally, I want to close with my latest offering, which is very special to me." With that simple introduction she began "Your Lying Arms," the song that had so convincingly assured her continued reign at the top of the music world.

The words of the song came easily as she slowly walked from one end of the small stage to the other. All eyes were on the lady, as her famous voice warmly embraced the room. She could look at no one as she told a story of love, lies, and deceit, things all too familiar to her in her most private moments. Out of necessity she stared over the heads of the audience to the back of the room. Her tears, many imagined, were just part of a truly great performance by a wonderful artist. Rhonda Haynes, indeed, conquered Washington that evening.

Conquering her feelings about Dusty had never been easy. That, she realized, might take a lifetime.

CHAPTER 24

August 7

Dear Rhonda,

    Yes, it's me. Don't wad this up just yet. Please let me say what I want to say. I'm sorry if you'd rather hear from the devil himself, but I had to tell you that I'm very, very proud of you. Not just your big evening tomorrow night at the White House, but for everything you've ever done since I've known you. You have always shared so much, and maybe that's because you have so much to give. I have never known anyone with a bigger heart. And I will always be grateful for everything you've done for me, every time you took me back, and all the times you gave me a reason to go on. My words wouldn't be anything without the meaning and the life you breathe into each one of them. And there will be more. I promise. Good luck tomorrow night.

Always,
Dusty